EMPTY BODIES

BOOK ONE OF THE EMPTY BODIES SERIES

Zach Bohannon

EMPTY BODIES
Zach Bohannon
www.zachbohannon.com

Edited by Jennifer Collins
Proofread by Christy McGuire

Cover design by Johnny Digges
www.diggescreative.com

"Zach comes out with suspense that will haunt you, and you won't be able to look away."
J. Thorn, Amazon Top 100 Horror Author

"Few horror writers work as hard as Zach Bohannon. Turn the lights low, and don't let the blood splatter hit you."
Dan Padavona, author of *Storberry*

"Bohannon's *Empty Bodies* is dark, enthralling, and offers an impressive look into a terrifying post-apocalyptic world."
Taylor Krauss, Horror Blogger

"Zach Bohannon takes dark thriller and suspense to a terrifying new level, with spine tingling tales of the macabre that will keep you turning the page deep into the night."
David J. Delaney, Author of *The Vanishing*

For my girls:
Kathryn and Haley

The beast that thou sawest was, and is not; and shall ascend out of the bottomless pit, and go into perdition: and they that dwell on the earth shall wonder, whose names were not written in the book of life from the foundation of the world, when they behold the beast that was, and is not, and yet is.

Revelation 17:8

CHAPTER ONE
WILL

Nashville, TN

The warehouse sat at the end of a long line of almost identical facilities; the last building on the left side of a single, inclined, dead-end road that was sixty yards wide and parted two rows of buildings. They were large, brick-front structures with foundations five feet tall—just high enough to keep *them* out.

On a normal weekday in the industrial park, the road would be a fury of semi-trucks backing up to loading docks, as blue-collar Americans inside the warehouses pushed boxes and drove forklifts, all in hopes of making a buck to live off of.

But things had changed.

Now, all the vehicles were vacant and still. Rows of cars sat where their owners had left them, parked to the top of the hill. Eighteen-wheel trucks remained backed into many of the docks along the street, but their cabs were empty, just like the cars.

And while the automobiles lay idle and the workdays were over, plenty of shadows still crept along the dead-end road. They walked up and down the street all day and all night, sometimes bumping into each other, but unaware of doing so. No life was left inside them, only the ability to make inarticulate noises and to hunt.

At the top of the hill, a large group of them loitered in front of Element Distributors; the company occupying the last building on the left. They gathered around it like it was a famous person, clawing at the cracked, brick walls.

Inside, Will Kessler looked out of a peephole that he'd made in one of the four aluminum, garage-style doors. He watched as hundreds of the creatures fought to get inside. They knew he was in there. He sensed that they could smell him. But Will wasn't worried. Standing over five feet tall, the loading dock seemed to make a good barrier between him and the things outside, as they had shown no ability to climb. His main concern was that he would run out of food, as he had very little.

Element was one of the country's top distributors of musical instruments. Since the late 1960's, their parent company in Belgium had been producing guitars and percussion instruments all around the world and, ten years ago, had opened a distribution office in Nashville, Tennessee. The facility consisted of a 30,000-square-foot warehouse with rows upon rows of metal uprights, crossed with matching beams, holding pallets of merchandise in each slot. Additionally, the building had an 8,000-square-foot office where twenty employees spent their days running the small company.

But Will was alone now.

Leaving the decrepit howls of the dead behind, he backed away from the doors, turned, and made his way back into the office.

***

Earlier that day...

Nearly every day, Will Kessler spent his lunches the same way: he'd go to the lunch room, make a turkey and cheese sandwich in the toaster oven, scarf it down, and then go to the vacant office across the hall and take a forty-five minute power nap. He was young, just shy of twenty-five, but working in the warehouse was hard work. Unloading forty-foot containers by hand and lifting boxes onto pallets all day wore him down. He'd often go home sore from head to toe, but because he was a night owl and suffered from regular bouts of insomnia, often sat in his room and played guitar. So, he was glad that the company had left one of the offices vacant when they moved into the newly-built office two months ago. The only thing in the room was a small desk with a computer for employees to use on their lunch breaks. Other than that, there was plenty of floor space for Will to snooze.

He was twenty minutes into a nap when he was suddenly awoken by a scream down the hall. He was sitting up before he knew he was even awake, and shot a sour look toward the door. The company consisted of thirty guys and no women—not on purpose, it's just that women never applied to work there—so there was always a lot of joking going on.

"Assholes," Will mumbled as he curled back up on the ground and closed his eyes.

Then he heard another scream. Much closer this time.

He opened his eyes and shot to his feet, just as he caught a flash of something going by the window at the front of the tiny office.

Will crept over to the window and, right as he was about to press his face against it, saw Dean, one of the guys who'd worked with him in the warehouse, hit the floor on the other side of the door. Will looked down and saw blood spraying into the air, out of Dean's arm.

As Will put his hand on the handle and started to rush to Dean's side, two figures pounced on Dean, who was only able to get a single yell out before one of the things tore his throat out.

Will thought quickly. While the two things were distracted, ending his friend's life in the worst way he could imagine, Will grabbed the desk from the middle of the room and put it in front of the door, making as little noise as possible. Then he stood in the dark corner, behind the door and out of sight.

His whole body quivered, his lips danced, and he waited. The silent air between the screams and the howls was filled with echoes of his heart beating in his chest.

Then he heard a slam against the window. He kept himself hidden in the corner behind the door. One of the things pressed against the window, trying to see into the room. Will heard it but couldn't see it. The snarl went into his ears and made him cringe.

Banging continued on the door. It sensed that something was inside the room. With nothing to defend himself with, Will's mind began to race about what he might do if the thing broke through the door. He looked to the exterior window on the opposite wall. There was no way of opening it, but if he had to, he could throw the chair through it and escape that way. But he decided that should be a last resort.

Then the banging stopped. He heard a voice down the hall.

"What the fuck?" the male voice demanded.

Will couldn't quite make out who it was, but from the Northeastern accent, it sounded like Mel, one of the sales representatives who traveled to the New England area on a regular basis, selling Element's products to local music shops. He was supposed to be on a sales trip, but had canceled it at the last minute, which now appeared to be the biggest mistake of his life.

Will heard a howl from the same voice and the sound of heavy footsteps moving down the hall, away from him and toward the voice.

He poked his head around the door to look out the window. It was clear. He walked over to the desk and opened the top drawer. *There has to be something in here to defend myself with,* he thought. There was nothing in the top drawer that would do any harm to anyone or anything.

In the second drawer, he found a Phillips-head screwdriver. *That'll have to do.*

The only plan he could think of was to try and make it to his boss' office near the front of the building. He knew there was a gun in there because his boss, a forty-year old outdoorsman named Andrew, was a card-toting member of the NRA, and had often bragged about keeping a gun at the office. If Will could make it there, he would at least have something tangible to defend himself with, assuming it was still there. *If* he could make it.

Will slid the desk away from the door, making as little

noise as he possibly could. Andrew's office was only about thirty yards away, but Will had no idea what he might encounter when he left the small office.

He closed his eyes. Took a deep breath. Put his hand on the door handle, pushed down, and pulled it toward him.

When he poked his head out the door, he looked to the right first and immediately brought his hand over his mouth to keep from yelling out.

Two more of his co-workers were on the ground with their entrails pouring out and hanging over their ribs.

He turned back into the room and emptied his stomach all over the carpet. After a few moments, he gained back his composure. Wiping the vomit from his lips, Will stood, hinged at the hips, facing the ground for a few moments before he remembered he needed to move.

His eyes went straight to Dean, his friend whom he'd watched get eaten alive just minutes before.

For a moment, he stood over him. Stared into his eyes. They were still open, even though he knew that Dean's soul had left.

Will picked his head up and stepped over Dean.

As he did, he heard the snarl and stopped.

A hand grabbed a hold of his ankle and he fell face first to the ground, letting loose of his screwdriver in the process. He clawed his hands against the floor and looked back to see Dean resurrected. Only it wasn't *really* Dean. His eyes had grayed, and intangible noises came out of his mouth. He squeezed Will's leg, chomping his jaws.

Will kicked his legs and turned back to look for the screwdriver. He could feel Dean spitting at him. He saw the screwdriver, but it was just out of his reach. Stretching as far as he could, he still couldn't quite reach it.

He felt his shoe come off and looked back to see Dean trying to pull his foot toward his mouth. In a panic, sweat dripping down his cheek, Will kicked his feet as hard as he could toward Dean. The grip on his ankle tightened.

Again, he reached for the screwdriver, and his fingertips brushed the edge of it.

He looked back and saw his foot moving closer to Dean's mouth.

At last, one of his kicks connected. Will's foot hit Dean square in the forehead, and the grip around his ankle loosened enough for him to crawl forward and grab the screwdriver.

He flipped over onto his back, sat up, and drove the screwdriver into Dean's left eye. Dean let out one last growl before the grip around Will's ankle became nonexistent.

Will lay flat on his back then, fighting to catch his breath. His stomach moved up and down like a flaying heart.

Down the hall, he heard a collection of howls echoing from the showroom.

"Shit," Will mumbled to himself.

He jumped to his feet and headed down the hall towards Andrew's office.

**

Behind him, he could hear the small horde tearing into another one of his co-workers, and wanted to move as far away from that as possible.

Without thinking, he went into the main part of the office. It was a very large room that extended to the exterior wall at the front of the building, with eight desks that the company's sales reps used lining the wall to his right. The middle of the room was wide open, and there were two additional large offices to the left, one of which was Andrew's. Will came to an abrupt halt as he realized the mistake of entering the room too quickly.

In the middle of the office, three figures were on their knees, mounted over a quivering body. He recognized their tattered clothes. It was three of the sales guys he'd worked with.

One of them, who Will recognized as having been Roger, looked back and hissed as he saw him. This got the attention of the other two.

Without hesitation, Will ran over and jammed the screwdriver into Roger's temple. The slimy sound it made as he pulled it out almost made Will throw up again. He held in what remained of his turkey and cheese sandwich and turned to jab the screwdriver into the next body. It was a new guy that Will barely knew. His first name was Ryan, but Will couldn't remember his last name.

The third one came at him and they tumbled to the ground together.

Flat on his back, working to push the weight off of him, Will was face to face with yet another co-worker, Emanuel.

He screamed, inches from Will's face, as saliva dripped down to Will's neck.

Right as he was about to bite into Will's cheek, he jammed the screwdriver into Emanuel's right temple. The thing became limp on top of him and his darkened blood dripped down onto Will's face.

He couldn't hold back his gut this time, and spilled it all over the floor once more.

***

Andrew shared his office with three other employees who held various operational positions within the company. A shape that almost resembled a human body, twisted and mangled, lay in the center of the office. While the smell made his empty stomach turn, the person was already torn beyond the point of coming back to life to attack him. It amazed Will how, in moments of survival, he had quickly adapted to seeing the dead. How he could move past them without blinking an eye.

Will ran to Andrew's desk and dug through all the drawers until he found the handgun. It had been a few years since Will had hunted deer with his father, and the weapon now in his hand reminded him of cool winter mornings, sitting in a treestand with his old man. He checked to make sure it was loaded. Of course it was. Andrew would never have had an unloaded gun at his side. What was the point?

Before walking away from Andrew's desk, Will picked up the phone.

"Damn," he said, as he put the dead phone back down on the receiver.

The next step was to clear the building and look for any survivors. The latter chance seemed grim, as no one so far seemed to have had the luck he had. Being lazy on his lunch break may have been the only thing to save Will Kessler's life.

He knew that a small group of at least two of his sick co-workers were in the showroom. He left his boss' office and headed back down the hall toward the rear of the building.

It was hard not to look down at Dean's body as he passed by it again. He knew that he had only been defending himself from the thing his friend had become when he'd jammed the screwdriver through his head, but it didn't make it easier.

As he continued down the hall, he passed the break room on his left. He looked inside and saw blood covering the table, the floor, and some more splattered on the wall. But there were no bodies.

At the end of the hall, he heard the rustling still coming out of the showroom.

Will put his ear to the door. As he'd suspected he would, he heard barking on the other side.

He held the gun up next to his face, drew in a deep breath, and swung the door open.

Three of them looked at him as he stepped through the doorway.

They stood less than ten yards away, and Will began firing rounds without paying attention to their faces. He didn't want to make it any harder than it had to be to put them down.

After he took all three of them out with consecutive head shots, he looked into their faces to confirm who else was lost. He was fighting to hold in his sadness, regret, and anger, but made a mental note: *Danny, Robert, and Jeremy.*

In the middle of the room, there was a large table that was used for meetings. Another one of his co-workers, David, lay on the table half-eaten. Will pushed his body off of the table, watching as his arms and legs landed, twisted through one another.

11

The room had two more doors. One of them led out of the office and into the warehouse while the other led outside, behind the building. Since he still didn't have a complete grasp on the situation, Will decided his best chance of survival was to clear out the building and hold things down here. So, he moved the large table in front of the door that led outside and then made his way through the one that went to the warehouse.

***

As the door swung open to the 30,000-square-foot warehouse, Will found himself alone. He could hear groaning and inhuman vocalizing off in the distance, but nothing in the corner of the warehouse where he stood.

He pulled another clip out of his pocket and popped it into the pistol, putting the gun under his shirt to mute the *click*.

With the gun now drawn in front of him, Will began to creep through the warehouse. Fifteen-foot-high racking running from the front of the warehouse to the back separated the space into eight aisles. The orange, steel racking that housed pallets filled with Element's products began twenty feet from the front of the warehouse and ended fifteen feet from the back wall, leaving an open, well-lit path along the back of the warehouse. And if things went south, he would have a quick path back into the office through the showroom door.

When he approached the first aisle, he looked around the corner.

Nothing.

As he moved further along the back of the warehouse, he

heard more snarls in the distance. The tongue of the inhuman, an adopted language of the new world.

The next few aisles had puddles of blood and matter on the floor, but nothing moved.

Will had to walk past four more of the eight aisles before he came across more of the dead.

Three people who had been his co-workers stood in front of him, their faces hardly recognizable now from the sudden change. These were men that Will had eaten lunch with almost everyday. But now, all of them were gone, their bodies left behind only to hunt him down.

Their backs were turned until the gun went off, which sent one of the creature's vacant brains all over brown boxes stacked waist-high on a pallet behind them.

The other two came at him and he pointed the gun at the one to his left. It was Jay, one of his fellow warehouse workers. Jay was only twenty-three, had gotten married four months prior, and had a child on the way. Will thought back to the day Jay had told everyone in the office that he was going to be a father. He'd been elated, going up to each of his co-workers individually to tell them about it. Now, as Will raised the gun to Jay's head, he couldn't help but remember the cheerful face of the father-to-be from that happy day, which now seemed so long ago.

He took a few steps back and looked into the other's eyes. His name had been Rick. He was the company's accountant, an awkward fellow that Will had never really gotten to know. Rick had been an introvert and kept to himself most of the time. They'd pass each other in the restroom from time to time, but didn't have to deal with each other much on a day-

13

to-day basis, as their jobs rarely called for it. The fact that Will had almost no relationship with the man didn't make it any easier to look into his eyes and put a bullet between them.

After Rick's mangled body hit the concrete floor, an echoing shrill came from the front of the warehouse.

Will ran toward the sound and saw one of the creatures straddling someone.

Someone who was screaming.

Fighting back.

Someone who was alive.

The identity of the person was hidden by a pallet of boxes.

Just as Will drew the gun, the creature got the upper hand in the struggle and dug its face into the stomach of its prey.

The person behind the pallet sat up, screaming, and Will saw the face. It was Jordan, a fellow warehouse worker who had become one of Will's best friends over their time working at Element. They hung out a lot on the weekend and spent many evenings after work drinking beers together at a bar down the street called *McKinney's Pub*.

"No!" Will yelled out.

The creature looked up and, even through the blood spread across its mouth, Will knew the face instantly.

It was his boss, Andrew.

Andrew stood and came at Will, who didn't hesitate to point the gun and fire a single shot into the head of his former boss.

As Andrew's body hit the ground, Will thought of every

time his old boss had been an asshole to him. Will thought of one specific time when he had shrink-wrapped a pallet of boxes too loosely, and when he'd moved it, the pallet had tipped over and the boxes had fallen all over the ground. Andrew had called all the employees to the front of the warehouse, pointed out Will's mistake, and demonstrated to the whole crew how to properly shrink-wrap a pallet. It had humiliated Will, and he had no remorse for the man lying dead before him.

His attention shifted as he looked down and saw Jordan's stomach open, his intestines letting go and beginning to pour over his ribs.

"Oh shit, Jordan," he said.

"Kill me," Jordan said through the blood coming out of his mouth.

Will just stared at him.

"Kill me."

Jordan turned his head to the side and looked away. His eyes welling, Will pushed the hammer down with his thumb. He still hesitated to pull the trigger, wondering how he had been put in the middle of this.

"Do it," Jordan mumbled.

Will saw Jordan close his eyes and begin to move his lips. He couldn't make the words out, but he assumed that Jordan —a well-devout Christian—was praying to God in his final moments.

"I'm so sorry," Will said.

The echo of the gunshot harmonized beautifully with the heightened cry from Will's lungs.

15

CHAPTER TWO
GABRIEL

Austin, TX

Laying on the desk on the other side of the room, the cell phone began to vibrate, startling Gabriel Alexander.

He rubbed his hair with a towel as he walked from the bathroom to the desk to grab his phone.

As Gabriel saw the name across the tiny screen, he smiled. "Hey, sweetie," he said to his wife, putting the phone on speaker so that he could continue to dry off and get dressed.

"Hey, honey. Are you still coming home today?" Katie asked.

Gabriel grabbed his brush and started running it through his black hair.

"I was planning on it. Is that okay?" He presented the question with sarcasm.

Katie sighed and Gabriel could hear the smile through the phone. "Of course it's okay," she said. "We just can't wait to see you."

The Alexanders lived just outside of Washington D.C. in the town of Alexandria, Virginia. Gabriel was a pharmaceutical sales representative and a large portion of his job was spent traveling. Katie was a stay-at-home mom to their twelve-year-old daughter, Sarah. His wife home-schooled Sarah and kept things running smoothly around the house since Gabriel had to travel so much.

"How's Sarah?" Gabriel asked.

"Good. She misses you. She was going to stay at Lindsay's tonight but I think she's going to stay home now. She really wants to see her daddy."

Gabriel smiled. Sarah was nearing the age where she would be *too cool* to hang with her parents. But she was a daddy's girl, and that would be hard-pressed to change.

He looked down at his watch.

"Look, honey, I gotta run. I don't wanna miss my flight," he said.

"Okay. I love you, Gabriel."

"Love you, too."

Gabriel hung up the phone and rushed to finish getting ready. He was already running late.

***

The tires of the taxi screeched as it came to a halt in front of the *Departures* area at the airport.

"That'll be $32.14," said the driver.

Gabriel reached into his wallet and pulled out a fifty-dollar bill.

"Keep the change," Gabriel said.

The driver's eyes widened and he stuck his thumb up.

"Thank you, sir! That is so gracious!"

Gabriel shot him a smile and a quick wave before hurrying out of the taxi. He grabbed his bag out of the trunk and jogged through the front door of the airport.

When he finally made it past security, Gabriel looked at

one of the monitors to check the status of his flight.

Flight 3427, Gate D, Washington D.C., Now Boarding

"Shit," Gabriel said.

He sprinted through the terminal with his coat over his left arm and his bag in his right, banging his shin with every frantic step.

In a dead sprint, he took a peek at his watch to check the time. When he looked up again, he saw a stout man standing in his path and it was too late to pivot and dodge him. Gabriel went shoulder to shoulder with the guy, tumbling to the floor. The man, much heavier than Gabriel, barely moved.

"What the fuck, asshole?" the man said.

Gabriel looked up, smiled, and waved as a way of apologizing.

The guy flipped him off and turned back to the woman he'd been talking to when he'd nearly been run through like a brick wall.

Gabriel hopped up and continued his marathon, running as fast as he could to catch his flight home.

***

The airline associate, a woman in her mid-thirties, was closing the gate as Gabriel barreled toward her, waving his ticket and boarding pass in the air.

"Wait!" he shouted.

The disgruntled woman looked to him, tapping her foot on the ground and sighing.

"I'm sorry, sir, the plane is about to pull away from the gate."

Panting, Gabriel shot the woman a desperate look.

"Please," he began. "I need to be on this flight." He pointed out toward the plane. "Come on, it's right there."

She sighed.

"Please. A beautiful woman like you isn't going to ruin this for me when I came this close, are you?" he asked, using his charm to woo her.

Gabriel was a good-looking man. As good as he looked in a suit, he could woo any woman with his business professional sex appeal.

The woman looked to the ground, shook her head, and laughed. She pulled a radio off her belt.

"I've got one more coming aboard," she said.

Gabriel hugged the woman.

"Thank you," he said.

She looked him up and down, admiring his physique through the well-fitted custom suit he wore.

"Guess it's your lucky day, gorgeous," she told him, eyebrows raised in approval of his existence.

He smiled at her, blushing.

"Guess it is," he said.

She opened the door to the tunnel back up for him and he walked through it.

"Do I at least get your name?" the woman asked.

Gabriel turned, walking backward. He smiled back at her, lifting his hand in the air to show his wedding ring.

She shook her head and rolled her eyes in disgust before shutting the doors and pulling the radio out once more to tell the crew inside the plane something else.

Gabriel smiled, approaching the door to the plane.

Another attractive woman met him at the door.

"Just in time," she said with a smile. "Welcome aboard the very lucky flight 3427."

***

Ten minutes later, Gabriel was settled into his chair, his luggage stowed away above his head and the plane fully populated around him. He could breathe easy now, knowing that he was headed home to his wife's homemade stir fry, and quality time helping Sarah with her math homework.

Abrupt rustling in the seat next to him brought him out of his trance. He looked over and saw a young boy; he couldn't have been more than ten years old, digging through a backpack and throwing its contents on the floor as he did.

Gabriel turned away and rolled his eyes, wondering just how thankful he really was to catch the plane at the last minute since he was now sitting next to an apparently unsupervised child. His thoughts went back to his family as he was able to relax and settle into the chair. Just as he closed his eyes, one of the flight attendants began to preach the airline's procedural script, the same one that Gabriel thought everyone on the plane had to have heard at least forty times.

"This is only the second time I've ever flown," the little boy said to him.

Gabriel looked over to him, giving him a nod and a smile.

"You should probably pay attention to the young lady up front, then," Gabriel replied.

"I've been staying with my aunt and uncle here in Texas. Now, I'm going home to Alexandria, Virginia. Do you know where that is?" the boy asked.

Gabriel sighed.

20

"No offense, kid. But I'm really tired. Not really in a chatty mood."

The little boy shrugged. He adjusted his cap on his head and reached into his bag, pulling out a candy bar.

One of the flight attendants, a tall and attractive redhead, showed up beside Gabriel.

"We all buckled in here?" she asked.

Gabriel nodded.

"And how about you, little man?" the flight attendant asked, looking over at the boy next to Gabriel. Peeking under the bill of his cap, he gave her a thumbs up.

The woman smiled and leaned over Gabriel to check the little boy's seat belt. Her perfume flowed into his nose, smelling like a spring flower and sending a chill through his nerve. He was a happily married man, no doubt, but it was hard to ignore this woman's beauty.

"All set, champ," she said to the boy. "What's your name?"

The boy looked up to her, cheeks red, possibly from seeing the beauty in a woman for the first time.

"Dylan," the boy said.

She smiled at him. "Well, Dylan. Go ahead and put that bag all the way under the seat in front of you. You can't have it out when we take off."

The woman gave Dylan a wink, clutching Gabriel's shoulder before moving to the next row.

As he looked out the window, Dylan swung his legs back and forth. He hit the back of the seat in front of him a few times, and the man sitting in it looked back to glare at Gabriel, as if the boy were his child. Gabriel ignored the man, turning his head away from Dylan, resting it against his seat back.

Within twenty minutes, the plane was off the ground and Gabriel was gone to the world, sleeping heavy in his chair.

***

The sound of gunfire woke Gabriel abruptly. He shook in his seat and gasped, looking around to make sure that everything was okay.

"Whoa, you alright, mister?" Dylan asked.

Gabriel looked over and saw the boy playing a handheld video game. He wasn't wearing headphones and the gunshots he'd heard came from the tiny soldiers on the screen. He put his palm over his forehead and let the back of his skull hit the chair, closing his eyes.

Feeling the sudden urge to use the restroom, Gabriel unbuckled his seatbelt and grabbed the seat back in front of him to help himself stand.

He narrowed his eyebrows as he moved into the aisle, now noticing how many people on the plane were coughing. A few rows back from him, one of the flight attendants was handing a bag to a woman, just in time for her to empty her lunch into it. The redheaded attendant came hurrying by Gabriel and he stopped her.

"Excuse me," he said. "What is going on with all these people?"

"Sir, we are doing our best to accommodate everyone. Please just have a seat and we will be landing shortly."

Clearly, the woman was in a panic. Her answer confused Gabriel, but he felt bad for her as she hurried to one of the passengers, throwing up in a bag like the other he had seen.

The ache in his bladder reminded him why he'd gotten up, and he made his way back to the restroom.

He went into the bathroom and locked the door behind him. As soon as he got his belt undone and his pants pulled down, he involuntarily began to relieve himself. He let out a sigh as the pain in his bladder went away. The stream flowed for what seemed like forever, and he looked around the bathroom that, maybe, one other person could fit in, as he daydreamed.

The urine finally stopped its flow, and he shook a few times to make sure that it was all out.

He felt a different kind of growl in his stomach. His bowels signaled to him that he had more business to take care of. He turned and sat down on the small toilet.

As soon as he sat down, Gabriel heard a slam and a collective gasp, which caught his attention. When all was quiet, he shook his head and went about his business for the next few minutes.

***

"Ma'am? Ma'am, are you alright?"

Dylan's hands lay as still on his handheld game device as the character on the tiny screen. He stared down at the friendly and beautiful redheaded flight attendant sprawled across the floor. The sound of the soldier being blown up by a grenade in the video game he had been playing made him jump, and he snapped out of his frozen state.

Looking around the plane, he noticed many people were standing with confused looks on their faces. Two rows ahead of him, a woman stood over a man, shaking him and speaking his name over and over. To his right, an older man

23

around the age of sixty sat slumped over in his seat. And beyond him, two more people looked similar, their limp bodies resting against the seats in front of them.

A male flight attendant whose face was blushed with concern was walking down the middle of the plane, attempting to calm everyone.

When he made it to Dylan's row, he asked, "Are you okay?"

Dylan shook, confused and scared. He nodded, but he wasn't sure if he *was* okay.

"Alright, just stay in your seat. Everything is going to be..."

The man let out a scream and Dylan heard the crunch. He looked down to see the redheaded flight attendant chewing the male flight attendant's ankle like it was a rawhide.

Then, the howls, barks, and screams escalated.

The muffled sounds of heavy artillery and bombs exploding disappeared as Dylan dropped his handheld game.

***

Right when he flushed the toilet, Gabriel heard the first scream.

His eyes got big as he pulled his pants up.

Then the screams became more frequent.

Gabriel reached for the handle and opened the door. He crept his head around the door and, just as he did, two people landed right in front of him.

He looked down to see a female flight attendant, lying flat on her back, screaming as the person on top of her began ripping her throat apart. Her eyes met his. Her helpless eyes.

Gabriel slammed the door and locked it, letting his body

lean against it to keep it shut as the screams continued throughout the plane.

"What the fuck was that?"

CHAPTER THREE
JESSICA

Somewhere in the Smoky Mountains—North Carolina

"But we reserved three suites, not one suite and two regular rooms," the young girl said. The frustration in her voice combined with her tone sounded like the voice of a varsity cheerleader, and was overshadowed by the smacking of the gum between her teeth.

Jessica Davies took a deep breath and gathered herself. The hotel had its share of bad customers. It was a resort for tourists, after all, sitting in the beautiful Appalachian Mountains atop a gorgeous overlook. It reminded her of the movie *The Shining,* its vastness and secluded location giving the hotel an ominous and haunted feel. Giant chandeliers hung from the vaulted ceiling of the lobby which was filled with elegant, inviting furniture, and was now full of people, as the hotel was headed into its busy season. With other guests anxious to check in, the last thing she wanted was to deal with a snotty bachelorette and her group of dolled-up and stuck-up-looking friends. She hoped this bitch wouldn't be her Jack Torrance.

"I do apologize, Mrs. Stevens," Jessica said.

The girl waved her finger at Jessica. "It's Ms. Brown. I won't be Mrs. Stevens for another two days and thirteen hours. Now, what are you going to do for me?"

Jessica's face turned red as she looked to the computer and confirmed that the reservation had been made under the name *Stevens*. The embarrassment showed on her pale face with ease. She was an attractive girl, only twenty-nine, with wavy brownish-red hair down the center of her back and big blue eyes. But living near the mountains had made her skin light with most of her time spent either in the hotel or in her room writing poetry. As a result, her face broadcast each of her emotions, much as she hated it in situations like this.

"As I have said, in addition to comping your rooms, we are going to provide each of you ladies with complimentary breakfast in the morning, and we will send two bottles of wine up to your suite shortly."

"Three bottles," the girl said, staring at Jessica as if threatening her, and continuing to flash her teeth through the gum.

Jessica let out a sigh, showing the hints of her frustration for the first time.

The girl put her hand out. "Whatever. Just give me the keys."

Jessica ran the plastic keys through the machine, coding them to their respective rooms, and handed them to the bachelorette.

The girl snatched the keys from Jessica's hand. "Thanks for not totally ruining my bachelorette party. We'll take that wine in twenty."

The girl turned to her friends. "Alright, ladies! Who's ready to party?"

The party hollered and cheered all the way to the

elevator.

Jessica put her palms flat on the counter and drew in a large, deep breath. She took both her hands and combed them through her hair to re-center herself before putting a smile on for the older couple who was next in line.

A woman in her early sixties approached the counter with an elegant smile. Beside her, a man who looked like he was dressed more for the beach than the mountains, wearing a casual button-up shirt with trees on it and a fisherman's hat, was looking back and watching the party of young girls walk away.

"I apologize for the wait," Jessica said.

The woman shooed her off. "Bless your heart. It's fine. No one should be treated like that. Right, Walt?"

The man ignored her, staring at the backs of tight jeans and yoga pants moving to the elevator.

She hit him on the arm.

"Okay, okay. Geez, Melissa," Walt said.

Melissa rolled her eyes.

"We are here to check-in. It should be under 'Kessler'," Melissa said.

Jessica looked at the screen, stroking data rapidly into the computer.

"Perfect. I've got you right here," Jessica said. "I'll just need the credit card used to reserve the room."

Melissa looked to Walt for the card. Again, he was looking toward the elevator as the bachelorette party loaded into it. Melissa grabbed his ear.

"Ouch," Walt cried.

"Give this sweet girl your damn credit card. You're gonna

kill yourself looking at that," Melissa said. She gave Jessica a wink, who smiled back at them, happy to finally have a friendly customer in front of her.

Walt handed Jessica the card. She ran it through the computer and handed it back to him, then prepared two plastic key cards, slipped them into a small envelope, and handed it over to Melissa.

"You're all set." Jessica pointed to the elevators. "You'll just head up those elevators to the 8th floor and your rooms will be down on the right."

Melissa reached out her hand and Jessica took it, shaking it gently. "You're a sweet, beautiful young girl. I wish my son could find a woman like you. Thank you."

Jessica chuckled. "Thank you, ma'am. You folks just let me know if you need anything."

***

After the early rush of guests checked in, Jessica stood at the front desk calling each of the new arrivals to make sure they had everything they needed and were enjoying their stay. When she came across the name *Stevens*—the bachelorette's soon-to-be last name—on the call sheet, she pushed a gust of air out of her lungs and corrected the name in the computer so that it read *Brown*. The last thing that she wanted was to call this girl, but knew it was part of her job. She picked up the phone and dialed *8-3-1* to call the room.

When the phone picked up on the other end of the line, Jessica had to pull the headset away from her ear. The music blasted through the earpiece, and the girls were hollering in the background.

"Yeah," the woman on the other end of the line yelled.

Jessica took a breath. "Hi. This is Jessica from the front desk. I'm just calling to make sure your room is okay and see if there's anything else we can help you with."

Again, Jessica had to pull the phone away from her ear. The girl was shouting something at her friend along the lines of she *couldn't believe that you would let him do that to you.*

"The room is okay, I guess," the girl said. "Hey, can we get some more towels and cough medicine or something up here? A couple of my friends aren't feeling well. It's probably from that dirty lobby or something."

The thought of girls in that party suffering brought a smile to Jessica's face. She only hoped that one of them was the gum-chomping bitch who was about to marry some unfortunate guy.

"Oh, I'm sorry to hear that," Jessica lied. "We will send some right up."

"And where is that wine you promised me?" the girl responded. "It's been a little more than twenty minutes."

Some of the smile slipped from Jessica's face. She knew now that it wasn't the bachelorette who was sick, only two of her friends. Still, that satisfied Jessica to an extent.

"I'll make sure that the wine comes up with the medicine. Anything else?" Jessica asked.

She heard a dial tone before she could get the last part out.

Jessica made a few more phone calls to happier guests and decided that she would take the wine, medicine, and towels up to the room. She could have had one of the bellboys take the items up to the room but, as much as she did not want to see the group of snobs again, she did want to get away from the desk and stretch her legs.

Steve, a newly-graduated college student who was a few years Jessica's junior, was working the morning shift with her. She walked behind the front desk area where he was grabbing a cup of coffee.

"I'm gonna go run something up to a guest," she said. "I'll be back in a few minutes."

Steve tipped his coffee mug to her and smiled.

Jessica started for the elevator.

***

Before heading to the 8th floor, Jessica used the service elevator to go down to the housekeeping office to grab some fresh towels from the laundry room.

The door opened and she walked across the hall into the office with the gold *Housekeeping* plate on the door. The hotel had an early check-in for special parties, and now the housekeepers were cleaning rooms before the three o'clock guests arrived, so the office was empty. Jessica walked over to the large metal sorting table in the middle of the room and removed a small stack of towels.

Closing the door behind her, she went down the hall to the restaurant's dry storage area. Scanning the wall of wine bottles in the large pantry, she grabbed one each of the cheapest bottles of merlot, chardonnay, and champagne she could find. Behind her, complimentary-size packs of toothbrushes, toothpastes, and various toiletries and medicines were displayed on two shelves. She picked up a small bottle of cough medicine and walked back to the elevator.

When the bell of the elevator rang and the display showed

the number *8* on the small screen, the doors split open and Jessica stepped out, immediately widening her eyes and letting her jaw drop.

The doors to most of the rooms were open while guests stood in the hallway shouting and panicking, some of them knelt over, and throwing up all over the carpet. Jessica dropped the cold medicine and the three bottles of wine, the glass shattering and the alcohol becoming permanently matched to the carpet.

Other people had begun to come out of their rooms, most of them screaming through covered mouths. Nearby, a man looked up from a woman lying on the ground and saw Jessica's hotel uniform. He stood and ran to her.

"You have to help me."

Jessica was overwhelmed. She saw his mouth move but was in a daze, like a flash grenade had gone off in the room and disoriented her. The man grabbed onto her shoulders and shook her, snapping her out of it.

"Please, help me."

"What happened?" Jessica asked.

Running his hands through his hair, the man said, "My wife. She began coughing when we got to the room. I thought she was fine. She said she just had a frog in her throat and to give her a minute. Then, she started dry heaving. I started to bring her into the hallway to get some fresh air, and she just collapsed."

"Is she breathing?"

The man cupped his hands behind his head and turned around. He was mumbling and wouldn't calm down to answer Jessica's questions. She walked over to the woman and knelt down next to her.

She appeared to be in her early forties, an attractive blonde. Jessica saw that the woman's eyes were rolled in the back of her head. Her chest and stomach were flat, and her arms lay still at her sides. Jessica reached down and grabbed the woman's left forearm. It was cold, the hand dangling at the wrist. She checked for a pulse.

"Is she okay?" the man asked.

"Stand back," Jessica demanded.

She leaned over the woman's face, tilting back the head, and then began to breathe into the woman's mouth. Jessica blew three deep breaths into the woman's mouth, and then clasped her hands over the woman's chest and began compressions.

For two minutes, Jessica repeated the process, all while the woman's husband stood muttering behind her. A few other people in the hallway who knew CPR were trying the same procedure on others with similar results.

Jessica again picked up the woman's arm and checked for a pulse. When she didn't feel anything, she set down the arm and placed her ear against the woman's chest. When she looked back up at the man, she had tears in her eyes.

"No! Please, God. Jennifer, baby, don't leave me," the man cried. He went down to his wife and straddled her, leaning over and running his hands through her hair. Jessica stood and took two steps back, watching the man come to the realization that his wife was gone

He looked up to Jessica.

"Please, do something," he pleaded with her.

Jessica covered her mouth and continued to cry. She

backed away, too overwhelmed by the panicked guests to know what to do next.

A scream bellowed from one of the rooms. Not the same cry of fear and despair that echoed through the hallway, but a scream of pain and utter terror.

Everyone in the hall fell silent. The cry had startled them, and they knew it was different. Something else was wrong.

A man with dark skin came tumbling out of the room that the scream had come from. He hit the ground face first, clawing at the carpet and leaving handprints in blood. He looked over at Jessica with bloodshot eyes and a face that she knew she would never forget. He reached for her just as another man came out of the room and pounced, lowering his head to the fallen man's neck and beginning to tear into his jugular.

Everyone still standing on the floor let out a harmonized scream and began to scatter.

Jessica heard a snarl followed by a scream just in front of her, and saw the blonde woman pull her husband toward her face and begin tearing his away from his skull with her teeth. Her eyes were red but pale, and she had a look on her face as if she wasn't really there at all.

The woman pulled away from the face to look at Jessica. She hissed and screamed at her, flailing her arms and trying to get the dead weight of her battered husband off of her.

As Jessica backed away, looking into the woman's eyes—this creature's eyes—she knew one thing:

The devil had checked in to her hotel.

CHAPTER FOUR
GABRIEL

Inside the small, isolated bathroom, Gabriel Alexander remained stranded with his back against the thin door. The screaming, howling, and banging around continued to ring through his ears.

On the other side of the door, he heard an extended snarl, seemingly directed at the metal he leaned against. He clenched his entire body, stood still, and tried not to make a sound.

A loud bang came at the door next to his ears. It startled Gabriel into a gasp, his body sweating from the absence of new air in the room.

Gabriel was unarmed. If the thing on the other side of the door busted into the room, he would be done.

A plunger sat upright next to the toilet. The room was small enough that Gabriel could simply bend over to reach it, leaving the weight of his ass against the door.

Once he had the plunger, he gripped it horizontally with both hands and brought the center of the wooden shaft down over his knee. He broke it just right, leaving a sharp edge at the broken end, thus creating a small, wooden stake for himself. He knew that he couldn't hold down in the bathroom for long, so preparing for his exit only made sense.

Gabriel rested the back of his head against the door and

closed his eyes, breathing deep as the monster behind him continued to slam its fist against the door and howl at him. He took one last deep breath and then moved away from the door.

It flew open and the thing, a woman, drooling from the mouth with eyes gone pale, came at him.

She pushed him against the wall and he dropped the wooden stake. They grappled, the woman chomping her jaws at Gabriel and spitting at him.

"What are you doing?" he asked, trying to push the woman away from him.

She was unresponsive, only growling and spitting at him. Together, they fell to the ground.

He was pinned against the wall, struggling with her. She worked to try and sink her teeth into his face, saliva pouring out of her mouth and landing on his cheek. As one, they fell over to the right, and his head slammed against the toilet. She lunged at his face, but he rolled out of the way, just as her face missed his and hit the wall.

Gabriel pushed her weight off of him and stood. He leaned down and grabbed the stake as she tried to get up, struggling to do so with her body pinned between the toilet and the floor. She managed to flip over, just as Gabriel brought the stake over his head and drove it into her stomach. She yelled out and kicked him back against the wall, still trying to get up.

He looked down at her, the woman apparently unfazed by the shaft of a plunger stabbing into her guts. Moving past her flailing legs, Gabriel put his foot on her stomach and pulled the stake out. She grabbed his foot and he lost his balance.

As he fell forward, all he heard was a slurping sound, and when he looked down again, he saw the stake poking out of her skull, neatly driven through her eye socket. She wasn't moving.

Gabriel looked down to her hands and noticed the paleness in them. He didn't know the woman, but no one was this pale. Her veins popped from the flesh and she was cold. Too cold for a body that had just passed. This woman, this creature, was human no more.

He put both hands on the stake and pulled, grimacing as the sound hit his ears, the stake slowly leaving her brain and carrying the remains of her eyeball a quarter of the way up its wooden shaft.

He set the shaft down onto the toilet and slid out of his sport coat, tossing it over the body of the dead creature, before picking the stake back up. Over the intercom, he heard the faint pleas of the pilot, urging everyone to stay calm.

Gabriel took a deep breath, held a solemn grip on the stake, and started out of the bathroom door.

***

The sheer chaos in the plane was a horror he could've never imagined. Down the middle aisle, bodies lay both sprawled and stacked on top of each other. On some, arms waved from figures who were covered with the bodies of the assailants. The lights flashed on and off above Gabriel's head and the captain was still working to calm down his passengers, apparently having no idea of the mutilation happening behind the comfort of the cockpit.

Then Gabriel heard a scream over the intercom, and the

calming of the captain ceased to exist.

Frantic alarms suddenly sounded through the plane and Gabriel lost his balance, grabbing onto a nearby seat to keep himself upright.

In front of him, one of the creatures looked up from its prey and saw Gabriel. It hissed at him from one knee as it dropped the head of its victim and stood.

The eyes, formerly a man's eyes, had gone as gray as a cloudy spring day. Blood covered its cheeks, and pieces of flesh were stuck around its mouth as it came at Gabriel without hesitation.

As Gabriel backed up, the plane began to rumble, sending him and his stalker both to the ground. The creature rolled over Gabriel, the motion of the plane sending it hissing over him and hurtling toward the back of the cabin.

When he was able to catch his balance, he looked back and saw the remains of his stalker's brains splattered on the wall.

He turned back toward the front of the plane just as another beast came at him. It was just about to bite his right arm when he blocked the path to his wrist with the stake, and the thing bit into the wood instead of his flesh. It chomped at the wood, leaving teeth marks in the middle of the shaft, as Gabriel pushed the beast away from him. They both fell backwards, away from each other, and Gabriel hit the back of his head on the floor when he landed.

He stumbled to his feet and limped over to the fallen creature. Looking over him, he saw those eyes. Those dead, cold eyes. They looked up at him without a soul. Remembering that the stab to the stomach had done nothing to his previous foe, Gabriel took the stake over his head, and with a thunderous plunge, drove it into the face of the monster below him. The blow covered his white dress shirt in a mural of red, but the thing's arms went limp and didn't move.

Gabriel put his foot on the chest of the beast and tried to remove the stake, but couldn't. The lights flashed and the plane shook again, sending Gabriel off his feet, banging his head again, this time against one of the seats. As Gabriel fell, he clutched his hand and grimaced, feeling the burn of a newborn splinter in his palm from the shaft of the plunger.

All around him, he could hear the echoing of beasts' howls and victims' pleas as the plane continued a turbulent and eventual fall to the earth.

The plane fumbled again and sent Gabriel rolling down the aisle toward the front of the plane. One of the things passed over the top of him, chomping its jaws and hissing as they passed each other in mid-air.

Gabriel stopped sliding and rolling as the plane leveled again. His face was against the ground and as he looked over, he saw the young boy curled under the seat in front of his. Dylan lay on his forearms and gripped the metal base of the seat, the lonesome helplessness flashing over him.

Gabriel knew that his only chance to survive was to get back into a seat and hope—pray—that none of those things got to him. He reached up, grabbed onto the nearest armrest, and pulled himself up into his original seat.

Dylan seemed unaware that Gabriel was there; he was in shock.

"Hey, kid," Gabriel whispered urgently.

The back of the boy's legs faced Gabriel and he continued to look straight forward, never glancing up.

"Dylan, right? We have to get you up into your seat," Gabriel told him.

Dylan still didn't respond.

Gabriel heard more screams from further toward the front of the plane, piercing through the pounding shriek of the alarms.

He knew there was little time, so he leaned over and reached for Dylan's legs.

The boy screamed and began to squirm, kicking back at Gabriel.

"Calm down," Gabriel demanded, but Dylan didn't.

His hands around the boy's stomach, Gabriel lifted Dylan off the ground as he continued to yell and, with his back facing Gabriel, slapped at whatever part of Gabriel he could find. Gabriel let out a groan, turned Dylan around, and slapped the boy across the cheek.

The squirming stopped and Dylan looked to him in shock.

"Listen to me," Gabriel said. "If you want any chance of seeing your mom and dad again, you better stop that shit right now and do as I say. Do you understand?"

Dylan, holding his face where the palm had landed, reluctantly nodded.

Gabriel guided the boy into the seat closest to the window and strapped him in. Above their heads, the oxygen masks swung back and forth. He grabbed the mask above Dylan's head and secured it to the boy's face, hoping that any beasts still alive were being bludgeoned by the plane's walls.

"Now, hold on," Gabriel told him.

Gabriel extended the seatbelt over his own lap and clicked it in, pulling to make sure it was secure. When he went to reach for his mask, the scream beside him stopped him.

A man, sick and decaying, reached at Gabriel. He was about the same height as Gabriel, but heavier by at least twenty pounds from what he could tell. Their hands were locked on each other's shoulders and Gabriel tried desperately to hold the thing at bay. Its mouth was open, spitting blood and saliva all over Gabriel, who screamed consistently, trying to fight the thing off.

Gabriel's hand slipped, allowing the thing to get within inches of his face.

Then, Gabriel watched its face fall back and away from him as the lights dimmed and the plane began to dive.

"Shit," Gabriel mumbled, his eyes wide. The plane was going down.

Frantically, Gabriel reached above his head, trying to grab the mask. His nervous hands shook but he found it and secured it to his face.

He took the hand of the little boy, who was screaming through his mask.

"Hold on," Gabriel cried out.

He closed his eyes, thinking of Katie and Sarah as the plane made its accelerated final descent.

CHAPTER FIVE
WILL

Though clearing the Empties out of the building had taken a mental and physical toll on Will, he knew that he had to keep others from getting inside so everything he'd just done wouldn't be for nothing. Before going back into the office, he moved two pallets, both stacked with product packed in brown cardboard boxes, in front of the two exterior doors at the back of the warehouse. They only opened from the inside, but it was better to be safe than sorry. With all the bay doors shut and locked, the two rear warehouse doors blocked with pallets, the door in the showroom at the rear of the building secured with a table in front of it, and the front door to the office barricaded with a few of the large desks, Will had secured every possible way inside, hopefully protecting himself from the Empties outside. He began moving all the bodies out of the main office and into the far corner of the warehouse where he wouldn't be able to smell them once they began to rot. He hoped he wouldn't be in the building long enough to have to worry about that, but moved them far away just to be safe.

He dragged the bodies from the main office first, watching the small lobby on the other side of the stacks of office furniture fill up with Empties who banged on the thick glass on either side of the door. While he was pretty sure that the glass would hold up, Will planned to spend as little time in that room as he could. If they made it inside, he wanted to be as far away from that room as possible.

Will moved Dean's body last, dragging it through the showroom and out into the warehouse, where he had an empty pallet waiting so that he could easily move the corpse to the far corner of the warehouse with the others. He used the forklift to move the pallet, and when he got to the far corner of the 30,000-square-foot warehouse, he tilted the forks, dumping Dean's body off the edge of the pallet and onto the pile of other corpses. Stacking the dead bodies did not seem like the most humane practice to Will, but it made the most sense to him; the only other option being to have bodies spread out over the building. Obviously enough, there would be no going outside to bury them. Will bowed his head and said a silent prayer for his co-workers before jumping back onto the forklift and driving up to where Jordan's body lay.

***

Jordan lay just as Will had left him: on his back, his head tilted to the side, mouth and eyes open, hands flat to the concrete at his sides. When he'd moved Andrew's body minutes earlier, he'd fought the urge to look down at his friend here, as he knew this moment would come soon enough.

He knelt down beside his fallen friend, whose face Will had covered with a towel he'd found nearby after he put him down. Will grabbed Jordan's cold hand and held onto it as tears came out of his eyes.

"I'm so sorry, man." He dipped his head toward Jordan's

hand. "I'm so sorry." They were the only words he could find.

Will's body shook as he turned his head toward an explosion outside.

"What the fuck was that?" he mumbled.

He hadn't heard anything aside from the banging and scratching at the doors, or whatever noises he'd made himself, so the loud crash outside made his eyes widen.

Will jumped to his feet and ran to the other end of the warehouse, through the door that led into the main front office.

When he looked out the front window, he had a perfect view down the street. He watched in amazement as Empties walked away from the building toward a large cloud of smoke that rose up on the horizon.

After staring for a few moments, he noticed it was too quiet.

He looked down at the ground outside in front of him, and there was nothing there.

Then he looked to his left at the lobby and, for the first time since everything had changed earlier that day, it was vacant.

They were gone.

He smiled and couldn't help but let out a laugh—the first one all day.

Was it safe to move the desks and go outside? He was hesitant at first, but could see both ways out of the window that it was clear.

So, he walked a few steps over to his left, slid the desk out of the way, and opened the door to the lobby. Moving quickly to the front door, wanting to open it and feel the fresh breeze brush against his skin, he still wisely hesitated, not sure it was safe yet to go outside.

Fuck it.

Will opened the door.

***

He stood at the top of the six steps that led up to the front entrance of Element and watched as Empties made their way down the hill toward the smoke; there were at least a hundred of them, maybe more.

To his left, he heard a rustle in the brush.

He drew the gun from the back of his pants, ready to fire, and crept down the stairs.

Element was at the dead-end of the industrial park and sat next to a line of trees. There was a small path between the building and nature to allow access to the back of the facility.

When Will stepped around the corner of the building, he saw what was making all the noise. One of them, a woman this time, had gotten her dress caught on one of the trees and seemingly been left behind by the others fleeing toward the smoke.

Will looked around to be sure it was clear. Then he just stared at her. He hadn't been this close to one without quickly putting it down and, for the first time, he got to see the fully transformed figure of the undead. She looked much older than she probably was. The blue polka dot sun dress that she wore gave him the impression she probably wasn't much older than he was. Weeks ago, if he had passed her in the industrial park, he may have even admired her, flirted with her. Now, her eyes were pale and her skin had a milky but decayed look to it. He could see right through those eyes.

45

Empty, dead eyes.

She let out a vicious hiss and he shook his head, snapping back into reality.

He drew the gun, cocked back, and then hesitated, taking a moment to think it through. The shot would bring at least some of the Empties back to Element. He reached down to his side and felt for the knife holstered to his side. While scavenging for supplies in his office, he'd found the large hunting knife that had belonged to his boss, Andrew. He wrapped his fingers around the grip, drew it from the holster, and approached her.

His mind began to race. He looked into her grayish-yellow eyes and knew she wasn't the same woman from her previous life. But he was hesitant to kill a woman; it was another taboo he hadn't yet crossed. The grip of the knife became loosened by the sweat in his palms. He licked his lips as he wondered if he could go through with it.

Then there was a tearing sound and he looked down at the bottom of the dress pulling away from the branch, distracted just long enough for her to be on him.

The spit wet his face as she snarled with her hands on his shoulder, working to get to his face with her decaying teeth.

He fell backwards and she came down over him, ready to strike.

As they were falling, her left arm moved off his shoulder just enough for Will to drive the large hunting knife into her left temple. Again, he found himself lying on his back with one of *them* on top of him.

He didn't have any more stomach to empty, leaving him in a heaving cough as he lay looking up at the dying sun with a dead woman on top of him.

***

While the Empties walked down the hill toward the explosion, Will decided to head behind the building to look for roof access, wanting to get an overview of the area around him.

Carefully, he peeked around the corner to the back of the building. There was another narrow path of grass between the backside of the building and more rocks and bushes. At the end of the path, with their backs turned, he saw two Empties walking around the opposite corner of the facility toward the front parking lot. Will kept still and quiet until they were out of sight.

The bottom of the ladder had a small cage around it that was locked from the bottom with a standard Masterlock. Will took the lock in his hand and pulled, hoping it wasn't latched all the way.

"Shit," he said as the lock didn't budge.

He thought of going back inside to find a hammer or a saw. Several tools were in the warehouse, but he didn't want to waste time in case Empties decided to return.

Against his better judgment, Will brought the gun up and pointed it at the lock. He figured, at worst, the two Empties he'd just watched pass around the corner would come back, and he should be able to take care of them with ease.

He closed his eyes and pulled the trigger.

A loud *clank* went through the air and Will saw small pieces of brick fly away from the wall.

The lock was gone.

He pulled the latch, opening the small hatch door. Put the

gun in the back of his pants. Jumped up to grab the bottom rung. Began to climb.

The snarls came from around the corner and the two Empties headed back his way.

Will looked at them for just a moment before turning back up to the sky and continuing his ascent to the roof.

***

When he reached the top of the ladder, Will pulled himself up onto the roof. He turned back and looked over the ledge to see the two Empties at the bottom of the ladder with their arms flaying in the air like two college girls dancing at a night club.

Will turned away and jogged to the front of the building and looked out.

No matter how much longer he lived, Will knew he would have the scene before him engraved in his head for the rest of that time. Years from now, he might even see the same image on a postcard, representing the frowning, depressed face of the new world.

Smoke had risen up around the skyline of downtown Nashville. The most notorious building in the city, the Batman Building—all the locals called it that because it had two antennas at the top that were higher than the rest of the building, making the top of it look like Batman's mask—was almost invisible from all the smoke. It was hard to tell if the smoke was coming from downtown or if it was just nearby. He wondered how many survivors were downtown, and if any kind of refugee camp had been set up, assuming that whatever had happened at Element had happened everywhere. Downtown was at least five miles away, so he didn't see himself getting there anytime soon. And for all he knew, he might be the last person on the planet, as the only person he'd seen alive was Jordan. He thought of the book *I Am Legend* and hoped that Richard Matheson wasn't right.

He turned his head to the left and noticed fire coming from a building that was closer by. From the location of the flames, it looked like the police station that was located on the main road, right outside of the industrial park.

Will looked back to his right, down through the middle of the industrial park, and that's when he confirmed there were over a hundred Empties in the park. Whatever had exploded and caused the smoke in the distance was attracting them all, though, and the area was clearing out. Some remained, but most followed the smoke.

Will looked down at his hands, palms flat on the ledge. He became overwhelmed by the moment then, and his heart sank. He realized that the world he knew was never going to be the same. He would have to adapt to the new way it was. Will began to think about his family. What were the odds that they had survived?

The dying sun was cooling the air, and Will sat down on the ledge and wept, passing images of his parents in his mind. It was the first time that he had let out all his emotion since everything had changed just hours ago. He reached into his pocket and pulled out his cell phone in hopes of contacting his mother and father. One corner of the small screen showed him that the battery only had 50% of a charge, and the other corner read *No Service*. He didn't even attempt to make a call. Instead, he turned the phone off and slipped it back into his pocket.

He laid back, flat on the wide ledge to watch the sun go down, thinking of his family and what he would do next.

CHAPTER SIX
JESSICA

Jessica shuddered at the scene before her, but quickly gathered herself. She was the only hotel employee on the floor and still had the responsibility to try and get as many people to safety as she could. Tucking away her fear as best she could, Jessica ran across the hall and pulled down the fire alarm, sending a wailing siren echoing down the hallway.

She scanned the hallway and was completely overwhelmed, having no idea how to help everyone. Jessica pulled the cell phone from her pocket and dialed *9-1-1*.

The speaker beeped at her. *Busy? How could 911 be busy?*

She looked down and saw him, the man she'd just watched have his face torn off by his sick wife, begin to move. While the skin on his face was torn away, his eyes moved around in their sockets as he tried to pull himself up. Even though they had turned pale, his eyes were the only things left on his face that made him resemble a human at all.

Jessica screamed. *How could the man be alive?* She had watched him be ravaged by his sick wife and stood there trembling as he drew his last breath. Now, he flailed his arms underneath the weight of his wife as she stumbled to her feet, still hissing at Jessica.

Jessica ran across the hallway, ignoring the atrocities,

and fled through an open door into one of the guest rooms. She shut the door, resting her forehead flat against it, and cried. Behind her, she heard more hissing. She turned to face the interior of the room and saw three people on all fours, leaning into the bodies of two other people and tearing them apart. She gasped as they looked back at her, away from their meal. Jessica fumbled the handle and finally got the door to open and moved back into the hallway—the war zone.

Jessica cupped the back of her head with her hands as she tried to breathe. There was blood everywhere as people were eaten alive all around her. She shuffled to her right, feeling as if she had nowhere to go.

From across the hall, one of the sick people began to groan at her. She was a woman, not much older than Jessica. Her blonde hair was still strangely radiant, though shining with the gloss of thick blood. Arms outstretched, she came at Jessica.

Jessica screamed, hoarse now from the repeated vocalizing, as she backed against the door.

Just as the woman was about to reach her, the door opened and Jessica found herself falling backward.

A set of hands caught her, pulled her into the room, and she yelled out as the door shut in the woman's face.

***

"It's okay, it's okay," Walt said, kneeling over Jessica. She lay on the ground in shock, flailing her arms and convulsing from her encounter with the dead woman and the graveyard in the hallway even as she looked up at the kind man in his tropical shirt, the fisherman's hat now removed to reveal his shiny bald head above a ring of white hair. Walt looked back to Melissa.

"Grab a cold towel," he told her.

He put his hands on Jessica's shoulders, working to try and calm her.

"It's okay, you're fine."

Melissa came behind him, dressed only in a robe from a recent shower, and handed him the towel, dampened with cool water.

"Shhh," Walt said to Jessica as he lay the cold towel across her forehead.

Jessica's arms quit swinging and her palms lay flat on the floor. She closed her eyes and now only fought to let her breathing catch up. The thudding in her chest persisted, but she controlled it a little more with each passing breath.

"It's okay," Walt said, dabbing the towel on different parts of her face. "Everything is going to be okay."

With a tremble in her voice, Jessica caught up with her rapid breathing enough to speak.

"What's happening?" she asked, looking back and forth between Walt and Melissa.

The banging on the door startled the three of them. It continued without a rhythm, sounding like the beat of a progressive rock band.

Walt stared at the door, but spoke to Melissa.

"Get dressed, now."

Melissa ran to her suitcase and pulled out the first set of clothes she saw, obviously not thinking or caring if they matched. Without hesitation, she dropped her gown to the floor, not caring if the young girl saw her in the nude, and put on a fresh set of clothes.

Walt stood and walked to his bag.

Irritated by the constant thump of the wooden door in her ear, Jessica stumbled to her feet, still slightly disoriented, and walked to the other side of the room.

Walt reached deep into his bag and pulled out a handgun. He pulled out the clip, confirming that the weapon was loaded, and snapped it back into place.

"What's the quickest way to the parking garage?" Walt asked Jessica, keeping his eyes on the gun.

The constant banging at the door distracted Jessica and kept her from thinking straight. She finally focused on her thoughts and spoke.

"There's a maintenance elevator, but it's at the end of the hall," she said. "It leads all the way down to the parking garage." She reached down to her key ring and pulled the key up to show him.

"Good," Walt said, looking back at her.

Jessica shook her head. "How are we going to get there? Have you looked out in the hall? It's suicide if we try to run all the way down there."

Walt shrugged. "We could be toast just as fast if we take the guest elevator and then the lobby is full of those things out there. And we sure as shit can't stay pinned up in here. May as well take our chances with a direct shot to a vehicle."

Jessica hesitated, then nodded.

Walt looked over to Melissa, who was dressed in a pair of leggings and a sweater. He threw her the coat lying on the bed and held up a small duffle bag.

"Put essentials in here. Your wallet, extra pairs of warm socks, and an extra pair of underwear or two. Nothing heavy." He looked down to her feet. "And put on your tennis shoes."

The banging increased at the door, sounding like more fist pumping. The hinges creaked like they could give away at any moment.

"We're gonna have to be fast."

The two women nodded.

Jessica walked to the door.

The view through the peephole showed four beasts beating at the door. Jessica pulled her face away and looked over her shoulder at Walt.

"Are you ready?"

Walt nodded. Melissa stood behind him, shaking, and gripping the duffle bag with both hands, the strap over her shoulder.

Jessica had no idea how she was going to get to the elevator with her present company. The couple was, at a minimum, in their early 60's. Walt had done his duty of keeping them safe so far, but that was in the confines of a small room and didn't involve any running. Even for her much younger legs, getting to the elevator would be a challenge.

Regardless, Jessica gave Walt a sign of acceptance. She removed the chain lock, turned the deadbolt, and pushed the handle down.

"Now," she screamed.

And the door to Hell opened.

***

The first shot exited the pistol, echoing through the room and sending the first sick person to the ground. Walt's aim was true. He fired at each of them from mere yards away, landing a blow to the head four shots in a row.

Jessica's eyes widened behind the door as Walt began to wave at her.

"Go! Go!"

Jessica followed his motion, moving swiftly through the door and into the hallway.

The gun shots had drawn the attention of more sick people from both the hallway and the guest rooms. As Jessica began to make her way toward the elevator, one of the beasts reached out to her. It caught her shirt, tearing it near the shoulder. Walt followed her out of the room and put a bullet into its brain. He put his hand on the small of his wife's back, yelling at her and urging her to run in front of him.

"Run! I'll cover you," he yelled to his crying wife.

And run they did. Down the hall they moved, dodging the grasps of the undead.

With adrenaline flushing his veins, Walt took aim and brought down any threat to either of the women, changing out the clip as fast as he could when necessary. The moment was surreal. It reminded him of being on the frontline in Iraq during Operation Desert Storm, never sure if he would be breathing through the next minute. When he fired the handgun at the limping, dead bodies, it was as if time stood still. Like everything had slowed down.

Melissa's vision faded as she ran, trying to block out the scene around her. She tripped over the mutilated body of what used to be a human, now rotting lifeless in the hallway, having been torn apart by the creatures.

Almost to the elevator, Jessica turned when she heard the fall. She hadn't realized how far ahead of the older couple she had run. Most of the sick people were behind them as Jessica looked on, watching Walt kneel down to aid his fallen wife. He looked up and waved at Jessica.

"Go! Get that door open," he yelled.

Trembling, Jessica turned and skidded the few extra yards to the elevator door. She fumbled the keys in her hands, dropping them on the ground.

"Damn-it," she mumbled, kneeling over to take the keys off the floor.

"Walt," Melissa yelled.

Jessica turned as she heard the groan. There was an ill person on Walt. Jessica's eyes widened as she recognized the outfit.

It was the snobby bachelorette, sick, and now turned into one of them. She had a hold of his arm as he screamed. He looked up to Melissa.

"Fucking run, Melissa! Run," he shouted, struggling to keep the bachelorette's jaw away from his skin.

She did, looking back every few steps with a river of tears coming down her cheeks.

Jessica looked to the wall and saw a fire extinguisher in a glass case. She went to it, pulled the case open, and removed the heavy, metal extinguisher.

Melissa arrived at the elevator and watched as Jessica ran to Walt.

The bachelorette was facedown on Walt's arm, tearing the flesh away from his forearm as he punched her in the head with his free hand. He heard a groan as Jessica lifted the fire extinguisher over her head, and with a scream, brought it down to the skull of the bachelorette with repeated blows. After the first hit, Walt was able to move what was left of his arm, and Jessica bashed the bachelorette's skull into the carpet.

Other creatures approached.

Jessica threw down the fire extinguisher, grabbed the gun off the ground, and took Walt's good hand.

Melissa was already in the elevator waving and shouting at them.

Walt groaned from the pain, but made it to the elevator.

Jessica looked down and started hitting the *PG* button, which stood for *Parking Garage*. The elevator took its time shutting.

"Fuck! Come on," Jessica yelled.

The door began to shut, just as one of the beasts reached out.

Its hand got caught, keeping the door from closing all the way. Melissa screamed.

Drawing the gun up to her face, Jessica pulled the trigger and heard the thing yelp as its hand fell to the elevator floor, and the door shut.

They watched the fingers of the hand move in their last reflex, the wiggling becoming gentle, as the elevator sent them down to the parking garage.

***

When they arrived at the Kesslers' minivan in the parking garage, Jessica and Melissa helped Walt into the backseat. Melissa sat in the back with him, taking the keys from his pocket and handing them to Jessica, who had made her way to the driver's seat. She cranked the van and adjusted the mirror so that she could see outside, but also keep an eye on Walt behind her.

Jessica backed the van out of the spot and drove toward the garage's exit.

They made the two-tiered climb to the ground level, and Jessica saw two sick people coming toward the truck wearing the uniforms of the valet boys. Being a front desk clerk, she knew them; it was John and Doyle, two friends of hers who played in a heavy metal band together when they weren't parking cars. Jessica hit the brakes.

Melissa looked up.

"Why did you stop? Drive," she said.

"I can't," Jessica responded.

She looked into their eyes. Her friends' eyes. Where had those eyes gone? But the closer they got to the van, the more she realized they were no longer her friends.

Melissa was crying. "Please, drive! He needs help," she pleaded.

"I'm sorry," Jessica mumbled.

She eased off the brake and pressed the gas, watching the two boys reach towards her as she ran them over, hearing the two thuds of their bodies as the van moved toward the sunlight shining into the garage exit.

CHAPTER SEVEN
GABRIEL

Just west of Nashville, open fields lay for miles across the long stretches of highway. Many of them, with grass so green from thriving in the rich soil of the delicate earth, housed acres of farmland and produced crops and food to feed the population. With many foods now being made in science labs and packaging plants, the land represented a dying art, one of the last memories of the blue-collar foundation of America. Out there, farmers could live off the land and sustain independence from the convenience of supermarkets and chemistry-created foods.

But everything had changed.

The Jacobsons owned the farm and, like the world, they too had changed. Left with no conscious minds to parade the sea of thought, they now stood in the open pasture, living off the land in a different way. Satisfying a new need.

They were a large family; nine of them to be exact, headed by the man of the house, Ron, and his wife, Rose. They had seven children, five girls and two boys. The second oldest girl, Rosa, was the one responsible for sending the house down in flames. When she rose from the ground following her sudden and fatal fall, she knocked a candle off of her nightstand, sending it onto the floor by her bed and catching the edges of her comforter on fire.

Three of the other children fell too, before resurrecting. The confused and mourning family never stood a chance. Not from the flames or from their dead children.

Now, the Jacobsons were nothing but frail minds moving aimlessly through a dead pasture.

The empty body of Ron Jacobson turned and looked up, growling as his attention was caught by the plane falling through the sky overhead. The carcass of the cow beneath him, lying motionless on its side, wouldn't be going anywhere. He had time—not that his vacant mind understood the perception any longer.

The plane continued its descent toward the field. An open flame shot off the rear tail and warmed the pale autumn air.

The other members of the Jacobson family looked up, each leaving the remains of the dead livestock they had slaughtered in the field. Roger, the younger of the two boys at eight years old, hobbled away from the carcass, attracted by the sound of the falling aircraft.

The scream of the plane heightened as it came down into the field, plowing over the Jacobsons' bodies and leaving nothing left to eat of the livestock, except perhaps scattered pieces of muscle, bone, and flesh.

On the other side of the field, where the tree line began, the plane finally came to a halt, having put the stolen minds of an American family out of their misery.

***

Gabriel opened his eyes and shook his head, letting his lips flap and making the sound of a horse carrying a shiver. He looked over to Dylan and saw the boy's eyes were shut, and he wasn't moving.

Gabriel quickly unfastened his belt and reached over, shaking the child.

"Dylan," he called.

The boy didn't move. Gabriel grabbed Dylan's thin wrist and checked for a pulse. Blood still flowed through his veins and the drum of the heart sounded through his body.

He looked around the plane and saw no movement. The only sound he heard was that of the engines failing and the gentle hiss of the flames flapping through the wind at the back of the plane.

Gabriel was scared to move Dylan in case he had sustained any injuries in the crash, but with the back of the plane on fire and not being sure if any of the sick people had survived, he saw little choice. He reached over and unbuckled the strap on Dylan's lap. Then he stood and leaned down, grabbing the dead weight of the child and throwing him over his shoulder. Dylan's arms dangled to the small of Gabriel's back.

He walked into the aisle and assessed the scene around him. Everyone and everything was dead. Bodies, or at least parts of them, lay all over the plane. All over the floor and all over the seats. The power was out, leaving the sunlight as the only illumination for the interior of the plane. Oxygen masks swung from above each seat. Aside from him and Dylan, no one had ever had a chance to even put one on. They were either ravaged and eaten by the undead, or left to be tossed around the plane like dirty clothes in an industrial dryer.

The plane had made a fairly clean landing, leaving Gabriel to wonder if the pilot was alive in the cockpit. He made his way there, stepping over parts of bodies in the process.

He reached for the door leading into the cockpit. It was locked. Gabriel put his ear to the door and heard a muted moan on the other side.

"Hello," he said.

He heard the groan again.

"Open the door. I can help you," Gabriel said.

He heard the muttered words but couldn't make them out.

One of the passenger seats near him was empty, and he sat Dylan down in it. The boy slumped over in the seat.

He stood back a few feet from the door and gave it a swift kick. To his surprise, the door opened on the first attempt, having likely been weakened during the pre-landing chaos and the crash itself.

With no weapon in hand, he crept toward the door, not sure what would lie on the other side.

Gabriel looked inside the cockpit to see the pilot still in his chair, leaned back with blood covering his uniform. Beside him, a body lay wearing the same uniform, face-first on the ground with a hole in the back of his head, and parts of his skull and brain scattered on the windows.

Gabriel moved to where he could see the face of the pilot, who jumped slightly as he looked to him.

"Did you land this plane?" Gabriel asked.

The pilot gave a slight nod.

"Thank you," Gabriel said simply.

A small laugh came out of the mouth of the pilot and was joined by blood.

Gabriel looked down and saw the missing square of flesh

from the pilot's neck. Blood seeped from the wound, and it looked alive as it pulsated. The hand of the pilot hit against Gabriel's left arm a few times and he felt something cold touch the skin on his hand. He looked down and saw the grip of the hand gun nudging at his palm. The pilot was nodding for him to take it.

Gabriel took the gun from the pilot and it felt even colder in his hand.

The pilot muttered something that Gabriel couldn't understand.

"What?" Gabriel asked, moving his ear closer.

"Me," the pilot mumbled. "Kill me."

Gabriel shook his head. He couldn't kill the man, even if it meant the pilot would be put out of his misery.

The pilot coughed and blood danced with saliva from his mouth.

His head turned and, eyes wide open, he was gone.

Gabriel looked down to the man's shirt and saw his name badge near a gold pendant that was in the shape of wings.

"Savage," Gabriel said to himself, mumbling the dead pilot's name.

He took the pendant off the pilot's white shirt and held it in his palm, wondering what kind of life this man had lived and who he had left behind.

Gabriel slipped the wings into his pocket and walked back through the door into the main concourse of the plane.

***

When he looked down at Dylan, Gabriel saw the boy's small left hand begin to twitch. He rushed to Dylan's side and put his hand on his forehead, running fingers through his bangs and checking him for a fever. For a moment, he felt like he was back home with his daughter, Sarah. His paternal instincts had kicked in with the young, abandoned boy, and Gabriel was treating him as if he was his own. But he was still left to wonder about the condition of his own wife and daughter.

"You alright, kid?" Gabriel asked.

Dylan's eyes began to open, fluttering. He took his hand and put his palm to the boy's forehead, the veins inside thrumming through his skull.

"Am I alive?" Dylan asked.

Gabriel laughed and smiled at the boy. "I think so."

He turned back quickly as he heard the growl come from the cockpit. Again, instinct kicked in, and Gabriel pulled the newly acquired gun from the waistband of his slacks. The weapon was still cold to the touch as he gripped the handle.

Gabriel stood, signaling to Dylan to stay put, and walked back to the cockpit.

He jumped back as he arrived at the doorway. Savage, the fearless pilot who had landed the plane and saved both him and the boy, was brave no more. He was dead, yet so alive. His eyes were bloodshot and his skin had gone pale. No words spewed from his mouth, only spitting growls. Still strapped securely into the seat, his arms were outstretched in a hopeless attempt to break free and devour the lives he'd saved.

Gabriel watched him from out of sight. No life remained in the man; he was a monster. Gabriel looked out the window and saw the endless trees just beyond where the plane had landed. In his mind, he was pretty sure that Captain Savage was dead—left only as a mindless creature aching to be released from the chair and wreak havoc. But another part of Gabriel Alexander wondered if the pilot could see the beauty in the trees in front of him. If he could treat them like a sort of gateway into an afterlife.

Gabriel pointed the gun at the back of Savage's head, cocked back, took a deep breath, and pulled the trigger, leaving the promising scenery of nature covered by a sea of red on the window.

CHAPTER EIGHT
JESSICA

"How is he doing?" Jessica asked, looking in the mirror and watching the tensed face of Walt Kessler.

Melissa had taken one of the extra shirts out of the duffle bag and created a makeshift tourniquet for his arm. The once white shirt was now forever stained crimson.

"I'm fine," Walt said before Melissa could answer, speaking in a way that tried to reassure the two women, but, to his wife, he'd come off more stubborn than sincere.

"Fine? Look at your arm, Walt!"

The fact that Walt even *had* an arm was a miracle. Jessica had gotten the bachelorette off of him just in time, before the sick girl had more critically injured him. A patch of flesh across his forearm, about the size of a post-it note, had been completely ripped off, exposing the tissue below but not quite down to the bone. When he twitched and his bicep flexed, you could see the muscle move through the wound.

"Really. I'm fine. You've stopped most of the bleeding, just keep pressure on it."

Melissa pulled the shirt around his arm tighter and he grimaced. It was almost more than she could bear to see her husband like this. She hadn't seen Walt hurt this way since he had come back from the first war in Iraq. Melissa rubbed his shirt in the spot where the scar from the shrapnel of a grenade sat on his stomach. Now, he would have a scar from a different kind of battle.

"Okay," Melissa said. "We are going to get you some real help as soon as we can."

But there was another problem.

The hotel was a mountain resort surrounded by nothing. There wasn't a gas station for ten miles down a winding road, much less a hospital.

And more than that, Jessica saw dark clouds in the distance. They were headed toward a storm. Rain would be no issue, but they were at a high enough elevation where sleet or even snow would be a possibility. The daylight was dying fast and, though the road had been safe and clear so far, they had no idea what could lie ahead of them.

Jessica eased the van down the curved mountain road, doing her best not to let her nerves veer them off the path and through the railing as the cold rain began to fall.

It took just over half an hour, but they reached a gas station. Jessica turned the wheel to her right and drove through the parking lot, stopping in front of the door.

"I'm going to go inside and see if I can get us help," she told Melissa.

Jessica opened the door and stepped out of the van. Dust kicked up beneath her feet as her soles slid across the dirt. She hurried around the hood of the vehicle and ran to the front door of the gas station as the rain began to fall harder.

***

The door swung open, sending the metal bells on the inside of the door clanking together in a fury of rings. It startled Jessica, the sense of abandonment instantly hitting her.

From the outside, the gas station had looked old and empty. There were only four gas pumps, and the signs looked like they would have only powered halfway on if there was power going to them. Jessica almost hadn't stopped at all, but the old pickup parked next to the store gave her hope that someone may be inside. And inside the store, the shelves were still stacked with product, and the floors, while not shining, were mostly clean.

"Hello," Jessica called out to the dead air. "Is anybody in here? We need help. There's a man outside badly injured."

Jessica waited for a few moments for somebody to call back, but it never came.

She walked down one of the aisles and found a small array of medical supplies. The gauze, tape, anti-bacterial, and mobile first-aid kits wouldn't do much, if anything, to heal Walt's wound with its severity, but it was better than what they had: a t-shirt.

Near the counter, a variety of tourist swag hung on a display rack, and Jessica saw tote bags with a cheesy picture of mountains screened on them, and text that read "Welcome to the Smokies". She grabbed four of the bags and began to fill them with as much stuff as she could. In addition to the medical supplies, she grabbed beef jerky, sports drinks, and bananas and apples from a basket near the front register even though they were starting to brown, and topped it off with various types of chips.

Before she walked away from the front counter, she reached next to the register and picked up the headset to the telephone. She let out a sigh and put the headset back down on the receiver as the line was dead.

She took the bags outside, placing them in the small storage area behind the back seat. Jessica then went back inside and, one at a time, took three cases of water bottles to the van, her hair becoming more cold and wet with every trip.

Melissa looked at her in confusion.

Jessica shrugged. "Place is empty. Don't think they'll miss this stuff."

She finished loading everything, then jumped into the back, sitting next to the cases of water. Melissa sat in front of her, behind the driver's seat, next to Walt's head as he slept. His breathing was steady, but he would gasp now and then, without waking himself.

Melissa pressed the buttons on her cell phone, disappointment mixed with panic across her cracked face.

"Are you getting a signal?" Jessica asked.

Melissa nodded. "Barely. Just not an answer."

"Who are you calling?"

"I tried calling 911 and I keep getting a busy signal. Just now I tried to call my son. He lives in Nashville. We were planning on going to visit him once we spent a few days here in the mountains." Melissa put her hand to her head and began to sob. Not only was her husband hurting in the back seat of their mini-van, but her son wasn't picking up his phone, leaving her with no confirmation if he was alive or dead.

"Do you mind if I try calling my parents?" Jessica asked. Her cell phone was sitting behind the front desk at the hotel, and she had no plans to go back and get it anytime soon.

Melissa wiped her nose with her forearm and reached over to Jessica, handing her the phone.

Jessica dialed her parents phone number, the only one besides her best friend Meghan's, that she knew by heart. It rang once, making her smile, before the three frantic ascending beeps led to the operator telling Jessica that the phone was disconnected. She looked down at the small screen and saw that the signal had disappeared.

Jessica grabbed the bag of medical supplies across from her, as well as a bottle of water for each of them. She reached over the seat to hand Melissa her phone.

"No luck?" Melissa asked.

Jessica shook her head and passed the bag and two water bottles over the seat to Melissa.

"Thank you."

"The only medical stuff I could find inside is in that bag," Jessica began. "I've got a little bit of food in the back, if you want to call it that. I also grabbed some sports drinks. Might be a good idea, if he will take it, to have him drink some to try to replenish some energy." Jessica squinted her eyes as she looked out to the open road.

"My parents live outside Knoxville which is on the way to Nashville. I say we head that way. You guys can drop me off there and then go look for your son."

Melissa gave Jessica a gentle nod and then looked back down at Walt, stroking his hair as he rested. He was old, but in this moment looked older. The color in his face had begun to flush.

"Hey," she said. Melissa looked up at her. "We are going to find him some help, okay?"

71

Again, Melissa nodded. She looked at the blood-coated shirt covering his arm. His eyes vibrated under the lids and his lips worked to match the rhythm. She knew that Jessica was trying to comfort her, but was unsure if it mattered.

Jessica looked out at the road and let out a sigh. "But it's not going to be tonight."

Melissa's face went cold and she looked back and forth between Walt and Jessica.

"What do you mean it's not going to be tonight? He needs help now," Melissa said.

Jessica listened to the rain patter louder on the roof of the van, stared out at the road, and then looked back to Melissa.

"The closest hospital is another hour's drive from here down this mountain. Before long, it'll be dark. It's pouring, and the roads up here ice over easily. On top of all that, we have no idea how bad things are out there, Melissa."

Melissa was angry. Deep down she knew that Jessica was right. Knew that they should wait it out. But her husband was possibly dying in her arms.

"This place seems safe. The power still works inside, so we'll have heat. We can lay Walt down somewhere flat and we will have plenty of water and food here. The van is already loaded and I'll put gas in it so that we can leave first thing in the morning without delay."

Melissa let out her breath. She stared into the back seat of the van, thinking.

"You're right," she mumbled.

"I know it's hard," Jessica said. "But there's..."

Melissa cut her off.

"I know. You're right."

Jessica cocked her head and looked around.

"We should get him inside," Melissa said.

***

Inside the gas station, they found a large storage room in the back to lay Walt down. Jessica grabbed some knock-off Indian-style blankets off of a rack and put them out on the floor, giving Walt something soft to lie on. They set him down first, then easily moved him back until his head rested on the blanket. He began to stir when his head hit the ground, but stayed asleep. Melissa grabbed one of the other blankets to cover him.

"I'll grab more blankets," Jessica said. "You guys can be in here. I'll stay in the main part of the store and I can keep watch while you both get some rest." She had taken the gun and put it in the back of her dress pants so that she would have something to keep watch with.

"Hey," Melissa said.

Jessica turned.

"Thank you."

Jessica smiled. "For what?"

"Helping us."

Jessica looked down at Walt and then back up at Melissa. "He's the one who pulled me in that room. He saved me."

Melissa smiled and a few tears made their way down her cheek.

"Hey. Do you mind if I try that cell phone again?" Jessica asked.

Melissa shook her head, reached into her pocket, and handed the phone to Jessica.

"Thanks. I'll let you know if I have any luck."

She turned around and left the room, heading out the storefront.

Behind the cash register was a stool with a worn leather top. She sat down and, again, dialed her parents phone number.

And again, nothing.

For the first time since the hotel, Jessica allowed herself to cry. For hours, she had held herself together, trying to stay calm for the sweet stranger who was watching her husband lie in pain. But in her new moment of solitude, Jessica decided to let it go. And like Jesus, she wept.

When the sun set, she found herself yawning. It had been one of the longest and strangest days of her young life, and though it was still early in the evening, Jessica decided to call it a night.

At the front of the store, there was a rack with various t-shirts on it. She grabbed one that said *North Carolina State Athletics* across the chest, unbuttoned her blouse, and let it hit the floor. She pulled the t-shirt over her head, and then reached under the back of it to unhook the clasps on her wet bra, pulling it out from under the shirt.

She found a spot on the tiled floor in front of the front counter, where patrons would normally line up to pay for their potato chips and gasoline. Two blankets were leftover and she laid one out flat, and used the other to cover herself.

Jessica lay there, alone, and all she could think about was her parents. Were they trying to reach out to her? Were they trying to get to her? And most of all, were they even alive?

Soon, she was dreaming about them.

CHAPTER NINE
GABRIEL

The sun had begun to fall, bringing a cooler breeze through the open field. It gave an ominous look to the cloudless sky, which rose above the downtown skyline, miles past the pasture where the plane had landed.

Dylan brought an additional blanket over to the body, leaned down, and lay it over the legs. He looked up to Gabriel with glassy eyes.

"Should we say something?" the boy asked.

Gabriel was looking at the wallet of Captain Leonard Savage. According to his license, he was fifty-three years old and from Baltimore. More than likely, Gabriel assumed that the flight to Washington was sending him home to his family —whom he also had a picture of in his wallet—a wife and two children in their late teens or early twenties.

He knelt down and tucked the wallet under the blanket, giving it two pats as he brought his hand back to the open air.

Gabriel kept his eyes down to the body and spoke to the boy.

"Yeah," Gabriel said. "I'll say something. Bow your head."

Dylan abided, bowing his head to the ground and closing his eyes.

Gabriel wiped his mouth and cleared his throat.

"We are gathered here today to celebrate the life of Captain Leonard Savage," Gabriel began. It felt awkward. Not only had he never given a eulogy, but he didn't know the man. Such honors were supposed to be for a friend or a loved one close to the deceased. To Gabriel, it just didn't seem right.

"He was a husband, a father, and apparently, one hell of a pilot." He cleared his throat again, peeking down at Dylan to see him still with his eyes closed and head lowered. "We thank him for landing this plane and saving us."

Dylan looked up. For the first time, he saw despair in the face of the stranger who had protected him during the crash.

Gabriel turned and walked away from the body. He stopped after fifteen yards and reached into his pocket for his phone.

"Shit," he mumbled to himself. It wasn't there.

"I'm hungry," Dylan shouted.

Gabriel turned around, putting on his best fake smile for the scared child.

"Me too," he said. "Let's blow this joint, shall we?"

***

There wasn't much to be salvaged from the wreckage. Gabriel wasn't even able to find his bag. He joked with himself that it was probably on a different airplane, knowing the reliability of the airlines, not to mention his unfortunate luck. However, they were able to find a gallon-size bag filled with miniature packs of peanuts. The protein in the nuts would be enough to tide them over until they could find more sufficient food, as well as hopefully keep Dylan happy for a little while. Gabriel knew that if he was hungry, the boy had to be as well, and would have less patience for controlling the pangs.

Gabriel stood outside the plane, waiting for Dylan to make his way back outside so they could try to find food and appropriate shelter before the sun went down, taking the light and little bit of warmth with it. He looked up to see Dylan emerge from the plane with his backpack over his shoulder.

"Lucky," Gabriel said, looking at the backpack.

"Didn't your parents always tell you to carry on your bags? Mine did. My dad said the best way to ruin my first flight was for me to lose my bag," Dylan replied, not an ounce of sarcasm in his voice.

Shaking his head, Gabriel turned and looked off into the downtown skyline. The sun was setting fast behind the buildings and he wanted to find refuge somewhere as quickly as possible. In the distance, he saw the black smoke coming off of the Jacobsons' farmhouse. The heat polluted the air, giving the skyline in that direction a foggy and dull appearance. In the foreground, a group of about ten people stood at the edge of the farm, stumbling back and forth behind a fence. From a couple of hundred yards away, Gabriel could tell they were no longer living, breathing, people from their poor posture and slight limp. These beasts were no threat to him and the boy, too far gone to know how to get past the fence.

Gabriel turned back around and looked through the line of the trees the plane had come to a stop in front of. They appeared to only go for a few hundred yards before light peeked out again on the other side. He squinted, sure that he could see something on the other side of the trees.

Looking down to Dylan, Gabriel pointed toward the trees. "Let's go."

Dylan put his hands around the straps of his bag as they left the plane and the large pile of a steel graveyard it had become.

***

After walking a few hundred yards unscathed, they made it past the edge of the trees and came upon the parking lot of a shopping center. It was the middle of the day and Gabriel was surprised to see that it wasn't busy. Normally, a shopping center like the one in front of him would be stirring with people. But now, it was calm, quiet, and abandoned. Gabriel saw a variety of stores in the mall, including two he would need to go into. There was a supermarket that he could only pray would have at least some food left, not totally raided by other survivors. Then again, he wasn't sure if there *were* any survivors. They hadn't seen any since the plane had come crashing down, even though they had only walked a few hundred yards away from a farm and through some trees.

A few buildings down from the supermarket was a sporting goods store. The captain hadn't left Gabriel with very much ammunition, so he would need to go there as well to obtain some more and, hopefully, another weapon or two. Again, Gabriel wondered if there would be anything left to salvage.

They moved a little closer to where they could see the other stores in the shopping center, and that's when Gabriel saw them.

He grabbed Dylan and ducked behind a nearby bush, putting his finger to his lips and signaling for the boy to be quiet.

There were at least twenty beasts limping around the lot and walking aimlessly around the abandoned vehicles. Gabriel wondered, even if he made it into one of the stores, how many more of the things would be inside. He looked down to Dylan.

"Stay right here, okay? Don't move," Gabriel commanded.

"No," the boy cried. "What did you see?"

"I'm not sure if I saw anything," Gabriel lied. "I just want to make sure it's clear before we go over there."

"Let me come with you. Please, don't leave me here," Dylan pleaded.

Gabriel shook his head. It was hard to look into the boy's eyes, his scared eyes, and tell him that he had to leave him alone for a little bit. All in all, he felt fairly safe leaving the boy there. They had just come out of the woods and not come across any danger, and the infected limping in the parking lot were far enough away where they would be no threat to Dylan. Regardless, looking into the boy's worn and tired eyes made Gabriel's heart slow and weep for him.

"Where are you going?" Dylan asked, wiping tears away from his eyes.

Gabriel pointed toward the shopping center. "Just right over there. I'm going to try to find us some food and a car."

He looked up and saw that the sun was dying fast. If he was going to do this, he needed to go *now*.

Gabriel reached down and pulled the gun out of the waistband of his dress slacks.

"Know how to use one of these?" Gabriel asked, praying that the boy had at least seen a gun.

Dylan nodded. "My dad takes me hunting all the time."

Gabriel let out a sigh of relief.

"Good. I want you to hold onto this. If you feel threatened, at all, I want you to use it. Okay? And then you run back to the plane and I'll find you," Gabriel directed him.

Dylan took the gun, shaking his head.

"I don't want you to go," the boy said.

"I won't be gone long. I promise. And when I get back, we are going to get the heck outta here and have food to eat."

The boy looked down at the gun before tilting his head back up to Gabriel.

"But what if you need this gun? What if someone comes after you?" Dylan asked.

Gabriel smiled. He rubbed his hand through the boy's hair and hinged at the hips to meet him face to face.

"In that case, let's just hope I'm still a fast runner."

Gabriel gave Dylan a pat on the shoulder. He could see the fear welling in the boy's eyes, and second-guessed himself on whether he should leave him alone. But in his gut, he knew it would be much more dangerous to take the child with him.

He removed his hand from Dylan's shoulder and stared down at him.

"Just remember to run if you get into trouble. Don't try to be a hero. Just run. As fast as you can."

With the tears continuing to gather in his tired eyes, Dylan gave Gabriel a nod.

Gabriel turned, closed his eyes, and took a deep breath.

He decided it would be best to try the sporting goods store first. He needed to find a weapon if he wanted to increase his chances of surviving. Unfortunately, the sporting goods store stood three suites further down the shopping center than the supermarket, creating a little bit further of a journey.

He scanned the parking lot again. The undead were spread wide through the parking lot, making it more difficult to find a gap to run through as a straight shot to his destination.

Once more, he took a deep breath. He thought of his wife, Katie; constantly wondering if she and Sarah were okay.

Gabriel opened his eyes and positioned himself into a sprinter's lunge—a funny sight, considering his current business attire.

He pushed off his back foot.

And Gabriel ran.

CHAPTER TEN
WILL

A couple of hours later, Will awoke, shivering. Fall nights in Nashville can get cold, and Will hadn't meant to fall asleep on the roof, especially on the ledge. When he woke, he startled when he realized that that's exactly what he had done, peeking over the side at a parking lot he could just vaguely see with the help of a couple of flood lights mounted to the front of the building.

He sat up, and as he looked down the industrial park and toward the city, he saw that very few buildings had power on. Beyond the immediate, Will could barely make out the smoke still floating in the distant air of the horizon.

For a moment, he stood still and listened. In the distance, he heard the howls of the undead, but it didn't sound like there were any near the front of the building, though he did hear scratching to the rear of it.

Will patted off the dirt on his clothes and walked to the other end of the roof, where the ladder was. He looked over and, while the ground was encased in total darkness, he could hear the Empties below, still clawing at the bottom of the ladder. It sounded like it was still just the two of them. He tried thinking of a way that he could distract them so that he could get down. It would be difficult to shoot them from the top of the ladder, and he didn't want to attract more of them, especially in the pitch black of night.

He looked around on the roof and smiled as he noticed the silhouette of a ball.

Many times while on their lunch break, Will and Jordan would go outside and throw the football around if the weather was nice enough. The last time they'd done it, Jordan was messing around and had punted the football onto the roof. Will was pissed at him at the time, but was more than thankful now.

He walked over and grabbed the football and walked back over near the ladder.

As hard as he could, Will threw the football into the trees that lined the opposite side of the building. The Empties snarled and walked toward the sound. Will hopped over the ledge and landed quietly on the ladder.

Slowly, he made his descent, trying not to grab their attention.

His feet hit the ground, rustling leaves. He heard them stop, turn, and the spitting came closer to him.

Will ran, moving around the corner of the building and praying that he wouldn't run into anymore Empties.

When he reached the front, the flood lights shined on a small horde coming at him.

His eyes widened.

Will hustled around the railing, his feet hitting the first step just as one of the Empties reached at him. It caught the bottom of his shirt, tugging it back for a moment, but he was able to move up the stairs and slip through the door, locking it just as the first Empty banged at the door.

He moved fifteen feet through the small lobby and went

inside the main office. The front door was locked now, but he still feared that Empties would break through the glass and fill the lobby again. So, as a precaution, he moved the office furniture near the door back in front of it. Looking out the window, Will noticed that a group of no fewer than ten Empties was making its way to the front door.

He wasn't going to be able to sustain himself here much longer. Meals would quickly become few and far between, only having whatever his co-workers had left behind. There wasn't a lot, as most of the guys ate out for lunch on a regular basis.

The time was fast approaching that Will would have to leave Element.

But, not tonight. He needed to sleep.

Will walked down the hallway to the lunch room, turning the lights off in the rest of the office to conserve power. His stomach grumbled and sounded like clothes turning over in a dryer, so Will looked into the refrigerator and grabbed deli meat and mustard to make himself a sandwich before going to sleep.

Earlier in the day while moving the bodies, he'd found a bunch of blankets that the company had purchased when they had moved from a building down the street five months previously. Will put several of them down to give his back some padding from the hard tile, and had enough to put over him so that he didn't have to run the heat in case it got cold and could conserve more power. After finishing his sandwich, he went to the center of the room and dropped to one knee to adjust the covers on his makeshift bed before moving under them.

As he lay on his back staring at the ceiling within his four walls of silence, Will passed the events of a day earlier through his mind. And the more he saw their faces, the more impossible it became to think about falling asleep.

***

Will awoke the next morning to the sound of failing machinery.

He sat up and looked around the room. The sound dissipated, and he listened close as it disappeared completely.

On the countertop by the sink, the microwave's digital display was blank. The previous night, he'd thought about unplugging it to save power, but had been too exhausted to move after he was under the covers.

The room sounded too quiet. He noticed the hiss of the motor in the refrigerator had gone away, and then jumped to his feet, hurrying over to it.

As he opened the refrigerator, he felt the cool air release, reached his hand in, and found that the air inside had warmed, then quickly slammed the door closed again. Reaching above the sink, he flipped the switch that should have turned on the garbage disposal. It didn't. He ran over to the light switch by the doorway and flipped it. Like the garbage disposal, nothing.

"Shit."

Will ran out of the doorway, down the hall, and toward the front of the building.

As he moved into the main office, the banging at the front door sounded louder. He approached it and saw a group of eight Empties, banging on the glass and the door inside the lobby. Behind them, the glass door of the main entrance lay shattered in hundreds of pieces on the ground.

Outside, he heard a different kind of banging, which caused him to turn.

He looked outside the window and noticed the parking lot was still mostly abandoned. There were some Empties out there, but they had started to walk away from the building.

The bang again.

Gun shots?

Will ran back to the lunchroom. On the floor was a duffle bag, which he grabbed and filled with granola bars and nuts that were left in the pantry and the last five bottles of water from the refrigerator.

He headed out of the small office, into the vast, open warehouse.

***

With the power out and no lights working in the warehouse, he crept carefully, only able to see a couple of feet in front of his face. The warehouse was eerie, quiet, and still. Will had ignored going out there for the most part, leaving it as a graveyard of sorts; a resting place for the suddenly departed.

If Will was leaving, it wasn't going to be in his late-nineties model Honda Civic. Instead, he remembered that his boss, Andrew, owned a large, dual-cab pick-up. Andrew always carried his keys on him, the dangling always sounding through the warehouse when he walked through to check on the employees, so Will knew they would be on his corpse.

Halfway to the corner, he could smell it. The rot. The decay. It was awful.

He pulled his shirt up over his nose, trying to block out as much of the smell as he could and holding back the sandwich he had eaten before bed the night before.

When he reached the stack of bodies, he saw Andrew's leg exposed, but not his waist where the keys would be. Dean's body lay on top of it.

Will reached out and began to roll Dean's body off of the pile. As he did, his shirt fell off of his nose and he instantly threw up all over the ground next to him. After that, he did all he could to get the keys as fast as possible.

And, just as he'd suspected, they were there, clipped onto Andrew's belt loop with a blue carabiner.

He unclipped the keys, gripping them in his palm like they were a talisman, and jogged to the front of the warehouse.

Jordan still lay in the same place he'd left him, with the same blanket covering his body. Will took the duffle bag off of his shoulder, set it down on the cold concrete, and knelt down beside his friend. He used his forearm to wipe the tears from his face, his sniffles slightly echoing in the large warehouse.

"I'm so sorry that this happened to you. I'll wonder every day how and why I survived. Was it just 'cause I decided to go on my break at a different time than you so that I could take a nap? A fucking nap saved me?"

For a few moments, Will remained there, knelt down next to his friend, allowing his tears to fall on his body. He rested his hand over Jordan's, which Will had placed over his stomach before covering him with the blanket.

"Goodbye, brother," Will said, taking his time to stand up.

***

Will stood at the peep hole he'd drilled into the large, aluminum bay door, looking out at the small group in the parking lot. From his vantage point, he could count eight Empties.

He double-checked his bag to make sure that he had everything he needed: food, water, a first-aid kit from the lunchroom pantry, and extra ammunition he found in Andrew's office. The gun was stuffed in the back of his pants, loaded and ready to fire.

Another explosion rang through the sky.

He looked out the hole and saw the group heading left toward the dead end of the industrial park. Will looked to the right where he could see another horde coming from down the street, where the exit to the park was. It didn't appear to be as many as he had seen on the roof. He assumed that the first explosion he'd heard had attracted most of that group.

With the power out, Will had no choice but to continue with his plan to exit. If he stayed, he would either freeze with no heat as the season continued its transition into winter, or he would starve when the food spoiled. He had to leave and try his luck elsewhere. He went to the shipping table and grabbed the small key that opened the locks to the bay doors off its hook.

Will made sure he had Andrew's keys in his hand, took a deep breath, and unlocked the small lock on the bay door, sliding it up and exposing the inside of the warehouse to the open air outside.

The small group that had been hanging around the outside of the building was about thirty yards away now, and the ones coming from the other end of the road were only about twenty yards away, leaving Will a clear gap to sprint to the truck straight ahead. The ones to his left were no concern, but the group coming toward the explosion had already seen him and started to snarl. He took a quick look up to his left and noticed the smoke coming from the tree line. He didn't know what it was and didn't really care. He only knew that he had to get to that truck. Fast.

Will took another deep breath and jumped off the loading dock. He ran toward the silver truck, hitting the *unlock* button on the keyless-entry. Nothing happened. He went to pull the handle and the door remained locked.

"Shit, shit, shit," he said, hitting the button over and over, trying to open the door.

A couple of *them* were moving closer to him.

He began to fumble the keys, trying to grasp the large black one, but his hands were shaking too much.

They were getting closer.

Will dropped the keys on the ground.

"Fuck."

He kneeled down to pick up the keys and heard the snarl behind him. He rolled on the ground, while the Empty fell down, arms outstretched, over the keys.

Will pulled out the gun and shot, taking off the top of its skull.

The shot gathered the attention of the group to his left, and they turned around and headed back toward him while the other group growled, growing ever closer to where he stood.

Will knelt down, closed his eyes, and rolled the decrepit body over to unveil the keys underneath. The skin was cold and gray and it felt like he was touching a corpse that had been buried for a thousand years.

Two Empties were just yards away from him now, and he turned and shot. It took four bullets, but he was able to put them down.

Putting away the thought of trying the keyless-entry again, he put the key into the small keyhole on the door and it finally opened. Will climbed into the truck just as twelve approached it.

***

He sat in the passenger seat and caught his breath. The banging began on the hood and sides of the truck then and Will knew his break was over.

He climbed over the center console and settled into the driver's seat. Still shaking, he managed to get the key into the ignition.

A crash came from his right as one of the Empties broke through the passenger side window.

Will cranked the truck and threw it in reverse. He heard a crash and then a pair of thuds, as he rocked from side to side, the back of the truck lifting slightly off the ground as it ran over a beast.

The growing horde walked in front of him, coming at the truck. He threw the column shifter into *Drive*, and punched the gas.

Two of them flipped over the hood on impact, putting a web-shaped crack in the windshield. With the passenger side window out, Will could hear the growls as he passed by the groups of them.

He zigged and zagged through the crowds, ignoring the herd as best he could, not wanting to do anymore damage to the truck. It was a heavy-duty extended cab and could take a decent beating, but he didn't want to add too much damage before he even made it out of the industrial park.

As he got to the end of the row of buildings and was about to turn the corner to head down the long stretch that led to the main road, something caught his attention out of the corner of his left eye. He looked over and his mouth spread open.

A young woman, around his age from what he could gather from the glance, was waving at him from the end of a loading dock. It was the first live face he had seen in days, and it was a pretty face; that much was easy to tell from where he sat.

He kept his eyes on her before he heard the cluster of snarls, and turned back to the road to see he was about to collide with a group of about ten. Will swerved; the corner of the truck caught one of them, and he heard the loud *bang*. The front left of the truck made a funny noise and the steering weakened.

Will had a flat tire.

The truck was slowing. He looked over his shoulder and saw the girl waving for him to come to her.

He turned the wheel all the way to the left and headed toward the building.

Will pulled up to the dock and the truck was quickly surrounded. A group of Empties had been loitering in front of the building when he pulled up, and they began to shake the truck back and forth, trying to get inside and rip him apart.

He looked up and saw the girl light an object in her hand and then throw it to a large, open spot in the parking lot.

The flare hit the ground and hissed, orange light shooting into the sky.

The group around the truck began to thin, and the driver's side door of the truck became escapable as they moved toward the flare.

At the loading dock, the girl widened her eyes and waved him to her more furiously, urging him to hurry up.

Will shook off his nerves, grabbed his bag, and opened the door.

He threw the bag into the building and put his hands up on the dock as she offered her hand to help him up.

Will took the petite hand and stood face to face with her.

She had brown hair with long, blonde streaks. Her blue eyes went right through him and reminded him of how thirsty he was from their ocean tint.

Still holding onto his hand, she shook it.

"I'm Holly," she said, smiling at him. "Holly McNeil."

Will smiled back, wondering if he was dreaming or actually standing in front of a real person.

"Good to meet you, Holly. I'm Will Kes..."

Will was out cold before he even hit the ground.

CHAPTER ELEVEN
GABRIEL

Dead bodies lay sprawled across the lot, emitting a stench into the air that was almost unbearable. Their blood was most visible over the painted yellow lines that designated parking spots at the shopping center. Unfazed by the decay, the undead lurked among them, splashing blood off of the concrete as they limped.

Two different times, Gabriel nearly slipped on something. He wasn't sure if it was blood or another substance from the human body, but somehow he kept his focus on the sporting goods store and on maneuvering a path around the loitering creatures.

The calculation he'd made near the trees of just how many of them were in the parking area was incorrect. He had estimated that there were twenty, but it was likely double that number. But he kept his focus, knowing that he needed to get to the sporting goods store. That he had to if he wanted to have any chance of seeing his family again and getting the boy, Dylan, back to his.

Gabriel should have been more focused on the ground in front of him. When he looked back to see how far he had run, he kicked the ribcage of a torn body sprawled across the ground in front of him, and stumbled to the concrete. He caught himself with his wrists and felt the pain shoot up his forearm as he landed, falling onto his elbow, both his knees, and rolling over. For a moment, he lay there on the ground, grimacing and rolling around.

Behind him, he heard the howls of the beasts.

He made it to his feet just as one reached for him, grabbed his shoulders and lunged its decrepit teeth at him.

They both tumbled to the ground, sending more burn into Gabriel's wounds as the side of his left knee hit the ground and he slammed his elbow again. He extended his arms, trying to push the thing away from him. He looked into its bloodshot, lifeless eyes as its mouth opened and it drooled down onto his face. Gabriel turned his head and could see more coming. With adrenaline running through him, he forced the creature—in its previous life, a man of around thirty years old from what Gabriel could tell—over onto its back and punched its face, which didn't faze it.

In a rage, he grabbed it by its hair and began slamming the skull into the concrete. It sprawled its arms through the air, trying to grab Gabriel—to stop him—but couldn't. Gabriel slammed the head until the skull cracked, and the thing stopped moving. He tried to catch his breath, but there was no time. More were coming at him.

Gabriel got to his feet and hissed as he felt the burn in his knee. He looked down and saw that his pants were torn at the knee, which was covered in blood. Nothing was broken or torn; it was just a superficial wound, but it stung. He re-focused his eyes on his destination and began to run again, doing his best to put the burn in his knee out of his mind.

***

As he arrived at the sporting goods store, Gabriel turned

around and saw that he had put a safe distance between himself and the undead. He reached for the door handle, taking a deep breath in hopes that it would open.

The door began to pull back, and Gabriel let out a sigh of relief.

Once inside, Gabriel turned and locked the door, leaning his back against the glass, and found himself sucking the dank air into his lungs. He looked to his right and saw a clearance rack knocked over, clothes and sports equipment sprawled on the floor. He noticed an aluminum baseball bat and kneeled over to grab it, taking the bat and pushing it through the two door handles at his back to give the door an additional barrier.

He turned and scanned the store for the first time. It looked liked a cold front had met a breath of warm air, creating a funnel in the middle of the store and tossing the product everywhere. Gabriel stood silent for a moment, listening for the hiss of any of the sick inside or, if there were any left, survivors.

Gabriel stood still until the bang on the glass behind him made him jump. He looked back and saw a group start to gather at the front door, groaning to get inside and tear him apart. The door was moving, but the baseball bat seemed to be doing its part in keeping Gabriel safe. He turned again and began to walk down the middle aisle of the store, sidestepping fallen goods as he moved.

The front part of the store was filled with clothes. He looked down at his and smiled, thinking that an athletic look might have to be the trend for him in the new world. Gabriel flipped through a still standing rack of t-shirts and grabbed one that had "LIVE TO PLAY" screened across the chest. He removed his tattered dress shirt, tossed it to the ground, and pulled the large cotton tee over his head.

A rack nearby displayed various styles of athletic pants. He found his size and swapped his torn slacks out for a pair of them. He started to put his shoes back on until he looked to the back of the store, seeing the entire back wall lined with tennis shoes. He smiled and threw his dress shoes down.

After trying on a few styles, he picked the most comfortable pair. He would have taken two or three pairs of the ones he liked, but he didn't see the point in carrying around a bunch of extra stuff. However, he did find it important to find a pair for the boy, as well as some extra clothes for each of them.

Nearby, a display stood against a wall holding an array of duffle bags and backpacks. Gabriel grabbed one of each, strapping the pack to his back and throwing the strap of the duffle bag over his shoulder.

He went back to the shoes and found a pair for Dylan that looked comfortable, and grabbed a couple of pairs in different sizes since he didn't know the boy's.

Then, Gabriel jogged back to the clothing section—the new shoes on his feet made running a breeze—and stuffed the backpack with an extra shirt and pants for himself, as well as some underwear and socks. He looked to his left and saw a collection of ski jackets on the ground. With the cold weather nearing, he needed one. He found his size, put on the coat, and zipped it up.

Gabriel hustled to the boys' section and found similar clothes for Dylan, including a warm jacket, and stuffed them into the duffle bag.

The banging on the front door grew louder as the crowd widened. Gabriel thought of Dylan, hoping that the boy was still in the same spot, awaiting his return. He looked through the window and saw that the darkness almost engulfed the light, and knew he was running out of time.

Jumping over more fallen product, Gabriel ran for the hunting section of the store.

The banging at the door continued to resonate and the sun continued its quick decline.

***

Dylan sat where Gabriel had left him on a patch of dirt, leaning up against a tree. He shuffled through his bag and grabbed a pack of the peanuts he had found on the plane, and split open the package so that he could eat them. The salt hit his tongue, bringing on thirst, but they hadn't found any water in the wreckage.

Bored, he pulled out his handheld video game, which somehow had survived the crash tucked deep into his bag. He powered it on, the small speakers sounding a jingle, and loaded his previous game.

As he sat there playing the game, engulfed in a make-believe war on a tiny screen, Dylan began to think of his parents. With no way to contact him, they had to be missing him. But what if they weren't? What if they were glad he was gone? His parents fought a lot, and like so many children caught in the middle of domestic disputes, Dylan often blamed himself. He wondered if, with him gone now, the burden of his parents had vanished. Either way, he missed them dearly.

He reached into his bag again and pulled out a photograph. It stayed with him all the time.

It had been taken during a family vacation in Myrtle Beach, South Carolina. They visited there often, as Dylan's mother was originally from there. They'd go there every couple of years and rent a large beach house, staying for the week with his aunts, uncles, and cousins. This particular photograph featured Dylan, both of his parents, and his older sister, Olivia. They stood at the end of a long pier, which stretched out over the ocean. This pier was one of their favorite places to go when in Myrtle Beach, housing an arcade for Dylan to play video games while the rest of his family would drink and listen to live music at the bar at the end of the pier. His favorite thing about the photo? They were happy. Both his parents were smiling, happy to be with their children, the exact way Dylan wanted to remember his mom and dad if he never saw them again.

A gust of wind blew by, and the picture sailed into the air, out of Dylan's hand.

His mouth opened as wide as his eyes, and he quickly dropped his game and ran after the photo, just as another breeze passed through and sent the photograph even further.

Dylan had moved almost thirty yards away from the tree when he finally stepped on the photo, keeping it from flying further away.

"Gotcha!"

As he bent over to grab the photo, he heard a snarl. He looked up, and saw one of the monsters limping toward him.

As fast as he could, he ran with the photo in his hand back to his bag. He tucked the photograph into one of the bag's secure side pockets, reached inside the main compartment, and pulled out the pilot's handgun that Gabriel had left with him. Grabbing his bag but leaving his game on the ground, Dylan turned and ran toward the plane, just like Gabriel had instructed.

Dylan tripped over a rock only fifteen yards away from the tree. He clutched his knee, wincing from the pain.

He flipped over onto his back, and watched the beast coming closer. It was alone, but relentless. Using his elbows, Dylan backed up, sliding across the mix of grass and dirt, until he was against another tree.

Sweat dripped down his face and his lips trembled. The gun shook in his hand, and he fought to take off the safety and cock the hammer back, just like his father had taught him.

It clicked, and the pistol was drawn.

But the creature was already falling toward him.

***

When Gabriel arrived at the hunting area in the back right corner of the store, the rotten stench stung his nose immediately. He walked around a corner, headed down one of the aisles, and brought his hand over his mouth and nose. Bodies—five, maybe up to eight; it was hard to tell—lay sprawled across the blood-stained tile. Some of the heads were still attached to their bodies and were either unrecognizable from the cannibalistic acts or had a gunshot wound in them.

Some weapons were missing from stock, but many of them remained. Gabriel was surprised that the place hadn't been completely looted. His best guess was that, whatever it was changing people into these limping and mindless beasts, it had affected enough of the people who were in the store that they'd simply overpowered the survivors—even with the barracks of rifles, shotguns, and pistols around them.

Gabriel walked to the glass counter. Rifles and shotguns lined the wall behind it and the case itself was filled with pistols, knives, and ammunition. As he approached the counter and looked over it, his eyes were quickly diverted in another direction. On the ground behind the register, a man wearing a red vest and a name tag lay dead, with a small family of rats picking away at his flesh. Gabriel turned and threw up all over the ground, landing knelt over and retching.

He gathered himself with a cough and a swipe at the mouth, and hopped over the counter. The rats squeaked and ran in different directions as Gabriel began to study the guns on the back wall. His eyes fell upon a black semi-automatic M4 assault rifle. He brought the gun off the wall and let the cold steel settle into his hands. He tossed the strap over his head and onto his shoulder, the gun meeting him at his hip. Next, he grabbed a pump action shotgun off the wall and threw it into the large duffle bag.

Gabriel turned and tried to open the case, but it was locked. For a moment, he thought about reaching down and trying to find keys on the decaying man before remembering the new world he was in. He smiled, then slammed the butt of the M4 through the case, busting it open and sending shards of glass onto the ground.

He grabbed two pistols, shoving one into the bag and mounting the other to his side, found the right ammunition for each weapon, and stuffed as much as he could into the two bags. As much as he'd hope Dylan wouldn't have to kill anything or anyone, he realized it was probably inevitable, and a pistol would be a simple enough weapon for the boy to handle.

Taking the M4 into his hands and loading it, Gabriel was thankful that his brother-in-law, Jimmy, was a military veteran who liked to take him to the shooting range whenever they would visit him in Georgia. It was there that Gabriel, a city boy at heart, had learned how to load and fire an assault rifle with some competence.

Gabriel started to turn away, but a large knife stared back at him from the bottom of the case. The handle looked as if his hand would wrap perfectly around it. He pulled the knife from the case, sliding it out of its sheath. As predicted, the blade felt perfect in his hand. It looked exactly like the knife that one of his movie heroes, John Rambo, would have used to butcher Vietnamese soldiers.

A crash came from the front of the store.

Time to go.

He threw the bags back on, much heavier now, and ran to the rear of the store to find an exit. A display caught his eye as he was about to enter the double doors leading into the warehouse. It was a free-standing display filled with Louisville Sluggers.

Gabriel smiled, grabbed one of the wooden bats, and ran through the back door just as the front of the store began to fill with limping bodies.

***

Like the rest of the building, the warehouse in the back of

the store was void of any life. Gabriel raced to the emergency door at the back, guided only by a few florescent lights that hung from the ceiling. A large red bar stretched across the metal door, and Gabriel assumed that once he opened it, it would lock behind him and there would be no turning back. He pushed through the door, sounding off the alarm just as the first swarm of dead pushed through the double doors behind him and into the warehouse.

Gabriel gasped as he walked outside. The light above the door shined on three monsters in front of him. They snarled as he stepped into the light, sensing the warmth in his blood. Not wanting to waste ammunition from the assault rifle, Gabriel pulled the pistol from his side and began to fire at them. The first shot caught one of them in the shoulder, only slowing it down for a moment. The second shot connected, hitting it between the eyes and sending it down. He started to jog away from the other two, firing, and connecting with the cheek of one of them.

He heard the alarm inside again as the back door of the sporting goods store opened. As they spilled out of the door, the siren was overtaken by growls.

Leaving the third creature to walk after him, Gabriel slipped the pistol back into the holster and ran, passing right by the back entrance to the supermarket.

His only goal now was to get back to Dylan and get the hell out of here.

CHAPTER TWELVE
JESSICA

Jessica gasped as the panic awoke her.

"Help! Help!"

She stood, leaving her makeshift bed of cheap gas station blankets behind, and ran to the storage room at the back of the building, behind the counter. When the door swung open, Jessica saw Melissa straddling Walt as he convulsed. His eyes were white, rolled into the back of his head, and his hips thrust with aggressive succession.

His lips were moving, and Jessica squinted and turned her ear toward him, listening close to him mumbling something almost indistinct.

"Get out," he said, under faint breaths.

Then, he ceased convulsing and his chest stopped rising.

Melissa looked up at Jessica with a blushed face, covered in tears.

"Please help! God, please help him!"

The only thing Jessica knew to do was to try CPR—a skill she'd been required to learn when she took the job at the hotel. She urged Melissa out of the way and put her head to Walt's chest, hearing a faint pulse. Her hands moved to his chest and she clasped them right above his sternum and began to perform compressions. After a series of pumps, she leaned down and breathed fresh air into his mouth, feeling his cold lips against hers and the coarse hair in his beard gone stiff.

Again, he mumbled something, and the volume was so faint, she wouldn't have had heard what he was saying if she hadn't been performing mouth to mouth.

"Get out of my head."

"What?" Jessica asked.

"Out." Walt closed his eyes.

Jessica repeated the steps two more times before Walt stopped moving entirely.

Her head lay against his chest and she heard nothing. The faded drum in his chest had stopped marching.

Melissa looked back and forth between her husband and Jessica.

For five more minutes, Jessica performed CPR. When all the color had flushed from his face and the beat in his heart hadn't returned, Jessica resigned.

Leaving tears on his shirt, she looked up to the still man's wife and shook her head.

Melissa cried out and let her entire body crumble to the ground.

Shoulders slumped, Jessica sat back onto her feet and wept for the man who'd saved her life and had now died because of it. She hardly knew the Kesslers, but such a debt could never be repaid, least of all now.

She stayed on her knees, watching Melissa clutch the cold hand of the man she loved, screams echoing through the small room.

***

Outside, the day hinted at more rain. Fog peeked over the

mountains and the sun lay still, hidden behind a cluster of clouds. It wasn't as cold as it had been the previous evening, and even with rain, Jessica knew she could drive them safely down the rest of the mountain. But for now, allowing Melissa time alone with the cold body of her dead husband seemed important, so Jessica waited outside. She sat just inside the open sliding door of the van nursing an orange sports drink. Every few seconds, she found herself looking down at the cell phone in her hand to see if there was a signal. It had become a futile routine.

Each time she checked the phone she thought of her parents. It was the most desperate of feelings, to wonder if they were alive. In her heart, she wanted to believe they were. But only reaching them on the phone or getting to them would prove that.

She stepped onto the dirt for a moment and moved into the front of the van, sliding through the doorway and into the passenger seat. Jessica inserted the key into the ignition and turned it over halfway to power the radio on, searching for a signal. Again, there was nothing.

She looked back as she heard a bellow from inside the gas station. Jessica grabbed the gun and left a trail of dust behind her as she hurried to the door.

Inside, she watched Melissa back away from the shut door of the storage room. Her hands covered her mouth and she was slumped over in disbelief.

"Melissa," Jessica said, getting no response.

Jessica tapped Melissa on the shoulder, flinching back as she turned and yelled out.

"It's okay. It's okay," Jessica said, embracing Melissa.

"Walt," Melissa cried into Jessica's shoulder.

Jessica gently urged Melissa away.

"What about Walt?"

Melissa wiped her eyes and pointed to the room.

Banging started on the door. It made Jessica jump, and her first reaction was to pull the gun from the back of her pants.

"No," Melissa yelled, pushing the weapon down toward the ground.

Jessica cocked her head.

"What's behind the door, Melissa?"

She knew the answer. But for some reason, she felt the urge to ask. Wanted to hear it out loud.

The banging continued until the wood in the middle of the door split open and a face appeared.

The eyes; they'd changed. No more the gentle eyes of the delicate stranger who had saved her life. The eyes were empty. Soulless.

Melissa began to reach out to Walt as he continued ripping through the door.

Jessica pulled her back.

"We have to go."

"No! I can't leave him!" Melissa said. Her mind was nearly as lost as her husband's.

Jessica's grip around her tightened as the older woman fought.

"It's not him, sweetie," Jessica said. "He is gone."

Half of Walt's body—one leg and one arm—were through the door. He was spitting toward them through hungry teeth.

Jessica began walking backwards, dragging the woman

who fought a little less with each step, but still reached after her husband.

Walt busted through the door just as they'd backed up to the front door of the store.

Jessica opened the door to leave, but Melissa put up one last fight.

As he got closer, Jessica drew the pistol and put three shots into Walt's chest. Melissa screamed out. When the bullets didn't faze him, though, she realized that the pale eyes were not of her husband; they were something else. She'd known all along, but fought to make the connection in her tired mind. It took watching Walt be shot multiple times in the chest for Melissa to comprehend that her husband was dead. She turned with Jessica and ran out the door, to the van.

Seeing the sliding panel door of the van already open, Melissa jumped onto the backseat.

Walt pushed through the glass and continued a powerful limp toward them, howling into the open air. His hat was gone, revealing his ring of silver hair moving in the wind.

Jessica slipped when she ran around the front hood, tearing open the material on the knee of her pants and leaving a scrape on her flesh in the process. She grimaced, but got back to her feet and slid into the driver's seat.

The key was still in the ignition and she turned it the rest of the way, hearing the engine roll over.

Walt reached the van and pounded his fists against the window of the sliding side panel door. On her back, with her head resting against the door on the other side of the van, Melissa looked into his dead eyes as he hit the glass. For a moment, she saw sadness and wondered if any part of him was left inside the pale eyes.

As the van pulled away, his eyes never left them. He limped behind them, arms flailing in the air as the sky opened and rain fell. Melissa watched him until he became smaller than one of the drops of rain.

"I love you," she mumbled, blowing him one last kiss before the van turned a corner around the mountain.

CHAPTER THIRTEEN
WILL

The cold rag against his forehead awoke Will in a stir. He opened his eyes and saw Holly with a look of concern over her face as she wrung the damp rag out in a bucket beside her. Her hair was up, making her eyes propel their beauty at him even more. He saw her full lips moving, but it took a moment for his ears to catch back up with his eyes after having blacked out.

"Can you hear me?" she asked.

Will shook his head to try and wake himself up a little more. He was sitting against a wall, his legs straight out in front of him, stretched across the cold floor. He tried to bring his hands up so that he could scratch his nose, but he couldn't. He rocked side to side, trying to remove his hands from the binding behind his back.

"What is this?" he asked Holly, furiously. He pulled on his hands, feeling the twine begin to rub his wrists raw.

She ignored him, dipping the rag back into a small bucket of water, and wringing it out, the sound of dripping water popping in Will's ears.

They were in a large, empty room with no windows. The floor was solid concrete and the walls were a pale white. Doors were on either side of the room. Will could only see out of one of them, but it appeared to lead out into the main part of the warehouse.

"What the fuck is this?" he yelled at her again.

"I'll tell you what this is."

The voice came from a man on the other side of the room. His boots clicked across the floor as he approached Will.

"This is your new home," the man said.

Will raised his head and looked the man up and down. He wore a fitted green t-shirt tucked into a pair of black slacks. He had medium length hair, dark and curly, and appeared to be in his mid-40's. From what Will could tell, he appeared to be fit, matched with a chiseled face under his beard.

"If you really want it to be, that is." The man spoke in a slight, but elegant, Southern drawl.

"Who are you?" Will asked.

The man knelt down next to him, working a toothpick between his teeth. He let the pick rest between his lips on the right side of his mouth, like a cigarette.

"My name is David Ellis," he said, sarcastically offering a handshake to Will, who shot him a frustrated look. David scoffed.

"Oh, yeah. Right," David said.

"What do you want? Why am I here?" Will asked.

David looked back at Holly, who was taking her hair down, straightening it out, and putting it back up in a ponytail.

"Holly, go grab Mr. Kessler here some water, will you?" David told Holly.

She walked to the other side of the room, flashing a flirtatious smile at Will, before walking out the door.

"How do you know my name?" Will asked.

David held up Will's wallet. "You can tell a lot about a man by looking through his bag."

David stood and began removing things from the bag, tossing them on the ground. He pulled out the pack of almonds and began to snack on them as he continued to talk to Will.

"We've been watching you," David said.

"I bet you have. You look like a fuckin' queer."

David smiled.

Holly arrived back in the room with a bottle of water. She knelt down next to Will and put the bottle to his lips, tilting his head back so that he could hydrate.

Will smacked his lips as they began to moisten, staring back at her, and trying to figure out the motive behind her glaring smiles and her kindness.

"The way you handled those people to get on the roof was impressive," David said. He reached down into the bag again and pulled out one of the bottles of water. Smiling, he showed it to Holly and shrugged.

Will swallowed his gulp of water and wiped his mouth on his shoulder. "What people?"

David pointed over his shoulder with his thumb. "Outside," he said.

Will laughed. "People? Those aren't fuckin' people. Not anymore at least."

David leaned in closer to Will and spoke in a firm tone with his Southern drawl. "What do you suggest I call them?"

Will put his head down and looked at the ground, not sure if he should say the word he was thinking. Then, it just came out. "Empties."

David cocked his head to the side. He flicked his tongue, moving the toothpick to the opposite side of his mouth.

"Empties?"

Will shrugged. "That's what I started calling them. They aren't really people. Their minds and their souls are gone. Not the people we know, not anymore. They're just empty bodies. Empties."

David laughed, and the toothpick moved up and down in his mouth.

"Clever! I love it," David said, sarcastically clapping his hands, which made Will glare at him. "We could use more people like you around here." He looked over to Holly. "Don't you think so, darlin'?"

She blushed and stared at Will. "That actually makes a lot of sense. Considering the fall and all."

Will looked confused. "The fall?"

Holly tilted her head at him. "Yeah, the fall. Didn't you see it when it happened?"

Will shook his head.

"Never mind all that," David said.

Holly blushed and ran her hands through her hair, a ritual she'd carried with her since high school and performed when nervous.

"So," David continued, "if you want to be part of my community, you have to earn it."

Will spit at David's feet.

"What if I don't wanna be a part of your gay little club?"

David brought the back of his hand across Will's face as hard as he could.

Holly gasped and covered her mouth, stepping back.

David looked back at her and gave her a stern look that told her to stop being dramatic.

Blood came out of the side of Will's mouth and he leaned to his right to spit some of it on the floor, as it was quickly collecting in his mouth. He moved his tongue around to make sure he wasn't missing any teeth. From what he could tell, the only one missing was the one he had lost when he was younger and playing ice hockey.

David grabbed Will by the jaw and came within inches of his face.

"You'll do what I say when you're in my house," David said in a demonic whisper. "Way I see it, you don't have much of a choice. See..." David pulled out a handgun and Holly gasped again. He looked back at her.

"Get the fuck out of here," David told Holly, using the gun to point to the door.

She left the room in a hurry and David turned back to Will, laughing.

He pointed to Will with the gun. Will dodged his head to keep the barrel from pointing at him.

"I think she likes you there, squirt," David said, smiling still.

"Fuck her and fuck you," Will said.

David ignored him.

"So, what's it gonna be? You gonna do as I ask, and earn your keep in this place?"

David pointed the gun right at Will's head.

"Or am I gonna have to blow your fucking brains out all over this wall right now?"

***

113

David shut the lights off in the room and closed the door behind him.

Holly was there, sitting in a chair and trying to gather herself. There were two others, a man and a woman, sitting at the table, and two armed men standing on the other side of the room, leaned up against the wall.

David walked over to Holly and slammed his hands down on the table.

"What the hell was that in there?"

Holly began to cry.

David put his hand on her chin and lifted her face up.

"You need to straighten that shit up," he told her. "We can't show any signs of weakness."

"Come on, David. Leave her alone. We're all still adapting and grieving from what's happened. Give the girl a break."

The voice came from the woman at the table. Her name was Diane Baldwin; she was one of David's higher-ups in his small community, primarily because she was one of the oldest members of the group made up of only about ten people.

David looked back at Holly, whose face was beet red. He gave her a soft slap on the cheek, then stood up and began to walk out of the room.

Holly looked up.

"Did you kill him?" she asked.

David looked back.

"Nah, darlin'. We need him."

***

Less than an hour later, light came through the door as it opened. Will raised his head slowly, squinting his eyes to readjust to the light. The bleeding in his mouth had stopped, drying up around his lips and the stubble on his chin, and leaving him with a sick feeling.

Two men who Will hadn't seen before approached him.

They leaned over and grabbed him, each taking one of his arms.

"Up you go," one of the men said.

Will grimaced as he came to his feet. He hadn't been on the ground *that* long, but it was solid concrete, and his hands were stuck behind his back. It made him feel as if he had been on that hard floor for days, and the joints in his knees and ankles popped as he stood.

They took Will into the next room, where he saw David, Holly, and a small group of others. In the middle of the room was a large, wooden table. The group sat around it, watching Will as he entered the room. David sat at the end of the table furthest away from Will. The two men sat Will down in a chair at the front of the room and then stood behind David.

Will looked to David with a blank stare on his face. He didn't let his gaze leave the so-called leader's eyes. David did the same, clasping his hands and leaning onto the table, never looking away from Will.

In fact, everyone in the room was staring at Will.

"So," David began. "Have you decided to play nice and do as I say?"

Will just continued to stare at him. All he could think about was that he'd had a clear path out of the park when he'd seen Holly's beautiful face as she waved to him from the dock, pleading for help. He was angry at himself for turning the truck around, wishing he had just kept driving, flat tire and all. Now, he was being held prisoner, forced to listen to some man pretend like he owned him.

"Let me just go ahead and tell you what I want," David continued.

He cleared his throat.

"Next door, there is a warehouse, much like this one and much like the one you came from. And it's overrun by those things."

"Empties," Holly added, glancing over at Will.

For the first time since arriving, Will smiled.

David glared back at Holly, who put her head down and took two steps back. Frustrated, he bit his lip, and started over.

"Next door is filled with *Empties*. We aren't really sure how many, but it's enough to have one of our men trapped."

Diane Baldwin sat at the end of the table closest to Will. She pulled out a photograph of a black man in his forties and pushed it in front of Will.

"His name is Marcus Wright," she said.

"He's my best man," David continued. "Yesterday, he went over there to scavenge the place and it was overrun. The girl with him, Claire, was killed."

Will interrupted. "How do you know Marcus is still alive?"

David held up a two-way radio. He turned it on and put it to his mouth.

"Marcus?"

The radio buzzed and Will heard another voice come through.

"Yeah? When the hell are you coming to get me, man?"

Marcus asked.

David smiled. "Soon. We'll be sending someone soon. Just hang tight."

He looked over to Will.

Will smiled. "You think I'm going to go over there, by myself, and save some asshole I don't even know?" He scoffed.

"Of course not."

The two men who had dragged Will into the room grabbed Holly from behind as she let out a surprised yelp.

"Your girlfriend is going with you."

CHAPTER FOURTEEN
JESSICA

For hours, not a word was spoken. The crying in the back seat had long ceased, turning into tired snores, while Jessica kept her eyes focused on the road.

The only things she could hear, aside from the old woman snoring in the back seat, were her own faint breaths and the echo of words she mumbled in her head as she thought about her parents. Since approaching the interstate, she'd come across both the living and the dead, though at times it was hard to tell them apart. She didn't stop the van. A few times she almost did, as seemingly innocent people waved her down, but all she wanted was to get to her parents' house. And she wanted to do so with a van full of water and food. She thought about her friend, Chris, who had been living in New Orleans during Katrina. Countless times, he'd told Jessica stories of how dangerous things had gotten when everyone in the city lost hope. No one was safe. The city of New Orleans had gone mad. And now, from what she could see, the entire world had gone mad, and there was no telling what someone might do to them if she stopped to help them.

An hour earlier, the radio had caught a signal and she was able to hear the message from the emergency broadcast system, warning people to stay inside. From what she could tell, most people were listening to the government mandate.

One thing that surprised her was how quickly she had become numb to the undead. There were stretches during the ride where she had to weave the van in and out of them as they moved with their arms swinging, down the open road. But they didn't cause her to cry or to panic. It was like she had lived in this world for a year or more instead of just a day.

She looked in the back seat as she heard the woman begin to stir. Melissa appeared in the rear view mirror with her palm pressed against her forehead as she tried to open her eyes.

"How long was I out?"

Jessica smiled. "We're only about thirty minutes from Knoxville."

"Wow," Melissa said, her eyes wide.

"You needed the rest, so I let you sleep."

Melissa looked around outside. They were driving down an unpopulated stretch of empty road.

"Have you seen more of *them?*"

Jessica nodded. "And people, too."

"And you didn't stop?"

Jessica shook her head. "Too dangerous. We don't know what people are like. I don't have too much faith in them right now, especially after listening to the radio."

"What did the radio say?"

Jessica reached down and turned the knob on the radio so that Melissa could hear the message.

This is the Emergency Broadcast System with an urgent message. The state of Tennessee has issued a house arrest

119

for all residents until further notice. Please be advised that no one is allowed outside until the ban is lifted. Failure to abide by these laws will result in instant prosecution. Again, do not leave your home.

"And when we crossed into Tennessee, there wasn't any resistance? No national guard or anything?" Melissa asked.

Again, Jessica shook her head. "Surprised me, too. I saw some military vehicles heading east about an hour ago. A whole line of 'em. But they didn't seem too concerned with us. Probably headed to Washington, if I had to guess."

Melissa leaned back and rested her head against the seat, peeking outside with her hand to her chin.

Jessica's eyes went to the dash.

"I need to pull over and put some gas in."

***

While Jessica tipped the plastic red gas can into the tank of the van, Melissa squatted behind a nearby tree and relieved herself.

"You didn't by chance grab any toilet paper at that gas station, did you?" Melissa asked.

Jessica laughed. "Wish I had."

Over the hill in the distance, a Jeep was moving west down the interstate toward them.

Seeing the vehicle a half a mile in the distance, Jessica pulled the can back, put on the lid, and loaded it back into the van.

"Melissa," she called out. "Melissa, we need to go. Someone is coming."

It was almost as if the person driving the Jeep heard her,

as it appeared to speed up.

Melissa came from behind the tree, buttoning her pants and scurrying to the van.

They weren't going to get away in time. Jessica shut the back door to the van and decided to play it cool. Maybe the Jeep would keep going. And if they did stop, maybe they would be friendly.

The engine of the Jeep calmed as it slowed.

"Let's just be cool," Jessica said.

She looked up and saw a man driving the Jeep, and that he was alone. He appeared to be in his early to mid thirties—not much older than her. As he pulled the Jeep in a few yards away from them, Jessica reached back and felt the cool handle of the pistol tucked into the back of her pants, assuring her it was still there.

The man opened the door and poked his head out over the roof, standing on the side rail of the Jeep. His eyes flashed to both of them.

"Everything okay?" he asked, the Southern drawl evident.

Jessica cleared her throat and faked a smile.

"Just fine," she said. "Just stopped to check the tires."

"And put some gas in?" He was pointing at the back cab of the van where she had put the can.

She cleared her throat and clenched her fists. Already, the stranger was making her nervous.

"Yeah. We got a little bit extra if you need some."

He nodded, rubbing the hair on his chin with his thumb and index finger.

"I see," he said. He looked over to Melissa and then back to Jessica. "This your mom?"

"Friends," Melissa said. She walked to the passenger seat and opened the door. "And we've got to get going. So, if you will excuse us..."

He put his hands up, stepped off the side of the Jeep, and then started to creep toward them.

"Whoa, whoa. Hold on a second." He moved closer to Jessica, who pretended to scratch the small of her back, though she had a firm grip on the gun.

He smiled at Jessica and said, "You told me I could have some gas."

She brought her hand from behind her back and signaled to the rear of the van.

"Yeah, of course," she said, faking a smile through a tremble in her voice.

He squinted his eyes at her. "What's behind your back?"

A drop of sweat came down her face. "Nothing."

He moved closer to her. His smile turned perverted and he bit his lower lip.

"You're pretty," he said, winking.

Jessica backed all the way up until her back was flush with the van. She began to tremble as the stranger reached out and placed his hands firmly on her hips. She could smell the chewing tobacco on his breath as his mouth moved closer to her face.

"Leave us alone," Melissa yelled, going to the back of the van.

He put the back of his hand up like he was about to slap her.

When he did this, Jessica pushed him away and pulled the pistol from her back, pointing it between his green eyes.

He put his hands in the air and flashed his toothless grin at her, again.

"Whoa. Put that down, sweetie. I don't want you to hurt yourself."

"I'm not planning on it," Jessica said. She pointed the gun toward his Jeep and blew out his passenger side front tire.

He looked back and dropped his jaw. Then he came at her.

"You stupid..."

The bullet entering his leg cut him off from finishing the sentence and he hit the ground. He rolled from side to side, clutching his right thigh where the bullet had entered.

"You shot me! You fucking whore!"

She pointed the gun at him again.

"Quit being a bitch," she said.

Melissa covered her mouth and let out a single, cupped giggle.

He writhed and watched Jessica walk to his Jeep. In the front seat lay a shotgun, a couple of boxes of shells, and a few unopened packs of beef jerky. She took the gun, the shells, and left him one pack of beef jerky. Before walking away, she looked on the back seat and noticed some paper towels sitting next to a couple of bottles of motor oil. She put those under her arm as well.

As she walked back to the van, she held the paper towels up for Melissa.

"Better than nothing," she said, thinking about the next time one of them would have to use the restroom.

Over and over, the man yelled "Bitch!" and "Cunt!" while continuing to roll around in the dirt.

As she stepped into the van, Jessica turned and put her middle finger up to the man.

"Thanks for the gun."

She blew him a kiss, shut the door, and kicked a cloud of dust into his lungs as she sped off toward Knoxville.

***

Just over forty-five minutes later, Jessica and Melissa arrived at the suburban neighborhood that Jessica's parents lived in on the other side of Knoxville.

The sidewalks and the roads were lined with the undead —about thirty were on the first street she pulled onto—but Jessica was able to avoid them without having to run any over with the van.

The condition of the houses varied. Some of them had doors wide open and windows busted, and they knew that these homes were likely now either vacant or filled with the dead. Others had boarded up doors and windows with lights on inside. The beasts were attracted to these, gathering in front of the doors and windows and beating on them with their fists.

"Think there are survivors in there?" Melissa asked.

Jessica nodded.

"Oh my God," Melissa added. The thought was in both their minds, that the fear they must feel while trapped inside their homes had to be driving them mad.

As they approached Ross Street where her parents' house was, Jessica's heart began to dance in her chest. It thudded against her ribcage like rising bread trying to burst out of a tight pan. She saw the name of the street on the green sign and turned the wheel to the left.

The Davies' house sat one block down on the right, and tears began to well in Jessica's eyes before the brick front home came into her vision.

Her mom's SUV still sat in the driveway and the doors and windows still looked to be intact. Ross Street was less crowded with the undead, and the front of their house was clear. In a way, it worried her more since many of the occupied homes they had passed had had beasts loitering in their yards. But she wouldn't know if her parents were alive until she went inside and saw for herself.

Jessica pulled the van through the yard, running over a small garden gnome, and parked it right in front of the door.

She took a deep breath, wiped her eyes, and opened the door to the house.

***

The Davies' home was dark and still as Jessica and Melissa entered. The smell of lavender still lingered. It was a scent that Jessica always remembered well from her childhood, as the air was infused by the potent oils her mom loved to burn. Her mom burned so much of it, in fact, that the oils had left a permanent stench on the walls and the furniture.

Jessica looked around and noticed that the house looked untouched. To her right, the furniture in the living room sat in its same respective places, not turned over and ravaged like she had feared. The kitchen to her left was spotless, aside from a small stack of dishes left in the sink.

Melissa reached over and flipped the light switch by the doorway, but nothing happened. Jessica heard the click and turned to look, as Melissa shook her head. The old woman hugged herself as the cold air hit her. She shivered.

"Mom?" Jessica called out. "Dad?"

No reply.

She walked through the kitchen and into the laundry room. The door next to the dryer led out into the garage, and she opened it. Her dad's red sedan still sat in the garage. Her heart began to race.

Melissa checked the living room, noticing all the photographs on the wall and on the tables. One in particular caught her eye. It was a picture of Jessica wearing a ballet outfit and laughing as her mom wrapped her arms around her from behind and tickled her. The picture made Melissa think of her son. She wanted so badly to get to him, and hoped soon that they would reunite. Though, she wasn't sure how she was going to tell him that his father had died. At least he would be proud knowing *why* Walt died.

Jessica entered the living room and a startled Melissa looked away from the photo on the wall.

"Anything?" Jessica asked.

Melissa shook her head.

"Did you check the downstairs bedroom yet?"

"No. Just in here."

Jessica passed the couch and hurried to the guest bedroom. Like everywhere else downstairs, it was empty.

"I'm gonna check upstairs," Jessica said. "Can you stay down here and be on the lookout?"

"For what?"

Jessica handed the pistol to Melissa.

Banging began at the front door.

"Shit," Jessica said.

She ran to the stairs as the howl from outside rang through the foyer.

***

The sweet scent of lavender faded into a musky overtone as Jessica climbed the stairs. Dying sunlight from outside shined in enough light for Jessica to see the faded fruit drink stain she had caused when she was nine years old, still embedded in the worn carpet on the fourth stair. The same pictures from her childhood remained nailed to the wall, unchanged and unmoved for years.

As she got closer to the top of the stairs, the scent got stronger. It stung Jessica's nostrils and began to make her nauseated. Her heart drummed with the beat of the door, as the beast continued to pound its fist against the wood.

Her parents' room was just to the right as she reached the top of the stairs. A nervous Melissa Kessler took turns looking to the front door and watching Jessica creep to her parents' room. She knew that the young girl needed to hurry, but she couldn't bring herself to push the issue. Not with everything that she had gone through herself today and how Jessica had been there for her through the whole ordeal. Grieving for her husband was something that would have to come in time. There was no place for it now, and Melissa feared that Jessica might experience a similar tragedy.

And as Jessica turned the cold handle to enter her parents' room, her exact fear was realized.

CHAPTER FIFTEEN
WILL

Will and Holly stood side by side in front of the large metal bay door of the loading dock. They could hear the Empties on the other side, spitting through their decrepit teeth and scratching at the door. Will felt a tap on his shoulder and turned around.

David held up a radio, offering it to him.

"Keep this on channel one," David said. "Marcus is stuck in a room near the back of the building, but this will help you get to him and stay in touch with us. He should be able to help guide you to where he is once you get inside."

Will took the radio and clipped it to his belt. He stared down at the rifle in his hands, thinking again about how he'd gotten into this situation. Wishing he had ignored the beautiful, and now scared, girl that stood shoulder to shoulder with him, about to take on a horde of Empties. And for what? To save some guy he didn't even know.

The rifle felt natural in his hands. One thing that he was thankful for was all the hunting trips that his father had taken him on when he was younger. His father had a friend who owned a plot of land near Manchester, a town about an hour and a half east of Nashville known only for hosting Bonnaroo each June, and from the time Will could fire a gun until he was seventeen years old, they had gone out there multiple times a year to hunt. Will had been raised with a gun in his hand and would have no issues taking down anything, or anyone, that threatened him.

He looked over to Holly.

"Are you ready for this?" he asked her.

She looked over at him. Her face was worn from crying and beginning to turn from a blush red to a pale nothing. She had a pistol in her hand that she hardly knew how to use and a knife holstered at her side. Holly was scared for her life, and Will tried his best to calm her nerves, even though he too was scared for their lives.

"We are gonna be fine. We will be in and out in no time. Just point and shoot like I showed you."

Holly took a look at the ground and then stared straight ahead again, waiting for the large door to slide up and reveal the dangers of the outer world. Though being under the control of another person—especially a dictator like David Ellis—was not an enjoyable life to live, the place they were in did provide a certain comfort. It had kept Holly and the rest of the group safe over the past two days. But now she was being put into a situation that she wasn't sure she would survive.

David patted them both on the shoulder and then turned around.

"Oh," David added. He waved his finger in the air at them. "If you try anything funny, these two will put you down. Got it? If you try and escape, I assure you that we have ways to find you. Now, go and complete your mission."

David moved to the other end of the room before turning around again. He crossed his arms and looked over to Jonas, one of his men who was standing by the door. He used his finger to signal Jonas to raise the door.

The light glared off the warehouse floor as the door opened, the screams of the Empties echoing inside the building. From the dock, the front door to the other building was about twenty yards away.

Will swallowed and wondered to himself if telling Holly that they were going to make it was nothing but an empty promise, a lie giving them false hope.

Outside, there were at least thirty Empties clawing at the edge of the loading dock. Their nails scraped the concrete, inches in front of Will and Holly's feet. Even though their lives were long over, Will scanned their faces and wondered about the lost clouds of memories behind each set of eyes. He wondered who these people were, what kind of lives they had lived, and if any of them deserved to be reduced to a limping nightmare. It was hard for him to fathom that *anyone* really deserved it. Even David Ellis.

Jonas stepped toward Will and Holly and pulled a road flare out of his back pocket.

"Ready?" he asked.

Will and Holly looked at each other, and then Will nodded his head at Jonas.

Jonas struck the flare, lighting it, and threw it across the parking lot.

It caught the attention of almost all the Empties, who turned and began to walk toward it.

Will looked back and saw David smiling.

"Good luck," David said, tapping his fingertips together repeatedly in front of his face.

***

With the Empties distracted, Will jumped down off the dock to the ground. He stuck his hand out, offering it to Holly. She took it and joined him in the parking lot.

They got the attention of a group of Empties that were scratching at the building next door, which they were headed to. The group of eight turned around and began to walk toward them.

Will brought the rifle to his shoulder, took aim, and looked over to Holly before firing.

"Remember to aim for their heads and to move quickly. When we start firing, that road flare isn't gonna do shit to help us."

She nodded and held the pistol up in front of her face. Her hands were shaking, and she could barely keep aim on the male Empty walking toward her.

Will had already looked away, cocked the rifle, and taken aim.

He took down four of them in succession, inhaling and exhaling to keep in control of every movement. When he looked over to Holly, he saw that she was still shaking and hadn't yet fired a shot, and that the Empty in her sights was moving closer.

"Shoot him, Holly," Will yelled. He could hear the snarls grow behind them as they were now about ten yards from the front of the building they were headed to.

She didn't shoot. Only remained frozen, except for her hands, which continued to shake, as the Empty moved closer to her.

As it reached out to grab her, the top of its head flew

through the air, landing on the ground next to her. She woke from her trance, looking over at Will, who had the gun pointing where the Empty had stood.

"Holly, I need you. Breathe, and shoot these fucking things."

She shook her head and raised the gun again, taking one hand off it briefly to move her hair out of her face. She wished she had remembered to put her hair up before jumping off the dock.

There were only three left in front of them. Holly's first shot went wide and the Empty she missed howled at her. Without hesitation, she fired another round and connected with a shot right in the middle of its forehead.

Will managed to take down the other two and looked back to see the horde behind them gathering closer. He reached out his hand toward Holly.

"Come on," he said.

Holly grabbed his hand and they sprinted the remaining distance to the front door.

Six steps led up to the door, and when they reached the top, Will looked back and saw David standing on the edge of the dock, clapping his hands and sporting an arrogant smile across his face.

***

When they walked through the front door, they entered an office with a layout similar to the one at Element. The power was out, leaving the only light to illuminate the space coming from the glow of the sun outside. Office furniture was scattered around the room, turned over like a tornado had swept through the inside of the building.

Will checked the room and saw that it was free of any immediate threat. He sat down in a chair and reloaded his weapon, looking over to Holly.

"I need you, Holly. Make sure you breathe. You can do this."

Holly stood in the middle of the room, nearly hyperventilating, with her gun down at her side. Her adrenaline was slowing down and the shock of potential death was starting to reach her mind. Will stood to put his hand on her shoulder and she turned to him.

"It's gonna be okay," he said. "We are gonna get through this."

Holly let her head fall into Will's chest as she began to cry. He embraced her, letting his hand run through her soft hair. Her warmth comforted him, especially in such a cold and dark moment. He let his fingers intertwine through her locks as his hand made its way down to her back to provide her the comfort of a strong embrace.

"I'm so sorry," she said.

"For what?" Will asked. He knew what she was talking about, but part of him wanted to hear her say it.

"Getting you involved in this," Holly began. "When I signaled you from that dock, David had a gun pointed at my head from the other end of the room.

"He has people that keep watch from the roof. They noticed you the other day when you went outside and took down some of those things. Ever since, David had someone keeping a close watch on you in case you made a move and tried to escape. He figured that you would after the plane came down and all the Empties started to move away from your building."

Will let go of his embrace and stepped back from Holly. "The plane?"

She nodded. "Didn't you hear the explosion?"

"That's what that noise was?" he asked.

She nodded. "Came down yesterday about the same time everything happened."

Will licked his dry lips. "Earlier you said something about a fall. What did you mean?"

After grabbing a nearby office chair, Holly sat down and took a deep breath. Holding back tears, she began to speak.

"I was in our lunch room grabbing some coffee. Rachel, one of my co-workers, walked in and we started having a conversation. She suspected her boyfriend was cheating on her, it was a big mess."

Holly let out a sigh.

"One thing that was kinda strange was this cough she had. The few minutes we were in there, she kept letting out this wrenching cough. I asked her if she was okay a few times, and she just waved me off like she was fine. I reached into the refrigerator to grab some half and half, and when I turned around, she was just lying there. I heard a gasp throughout the building. When I kneeled down to help her, she wasn't breathing. So I ran out of the lunch room to get help.

"When I left the room, I saw that Rachel wasn't the only one who had fallen. Almost everyone in the office had. A few other people were performing CPR. One of them was Bruce, our accountant. He pointed at me and asked me to call 911."

She began to cry now, and Will put his hand on her

shoulder, which she clutched for comfort.

"The line was busy. Craziest thing I ever experienced. How could 911 be busy? Then I heard the first screams."

She was crying more now and couldn't describe what she saw. But she didn't have to. The story resembled Will's all too well.

"I locked myself in the office and just watched. Marcus, the guy we are going after, is the one that finally came and got me out of there. I don't even remember how much time had passed. Twenty, maybe thirty minutes? It seemed like hours."

She wiped her face and cleared her throat, still holding tight onto Will's hand.

"Apparently, everyone fell. That's why I said that calling them 'Empties' made a lot of sense to me. They aren't the same people. It seems exactly like you said: that their souls were taken."

For the first time during the conversation, Holly looked up from the ground into Will's eyes.

"It's almost like it was an act of God."

It hung in the air for a few moments before Will changed the subject.

"Who is David?" Will asked.

Holly handed her pistol to Will so that he could reload it. She pulled a hair tie out of her pocket and began to put her hair up. Will noticed how her breasts collected in the V-neck of her tank top she wore under the green jacket as she lifted her arms.

"He owns these buildings," she said. "This building and the other one, they're one company. The company is a metal heat-treating facility. We all worked here. David just happened to be here in town from St. Louis when all this shit started happening. He always comes here this time of year to check on the business and to go hunting. That's why he has all those weapons. The man brings a fucking arsenal with him just to go out and kill Bambi." She licked her lips. "Marcus, the guy we are here to find, was the plant manager at this location and a huge suck-up to David. I think he only does it because he has to. He's a really good guy, and David actually cares for him a lot."

She looked up at him.

"They're all loyal to him. They think that he's going to get us out of this mess. It's bullshit. He's a rich, control-hungry, smug, asshole. And he's using this situation to try and become some kind of dictator or saint, as he thinks."

Will's face went cold. He knew that going back to David wasn't the ideal situation, but trying to escape and not going back would be much worse. All he needed was some loyal, cult-following assassins coming after him and Holly.

"I don't wanna go back there," she said.

Will stood and looked down at her. "We have to. But we won't be staying long when we do."

She cocked her head slightly at him.

The radio at Will's waist let out a static hiss.

"What's going on? Are you guys there?"

It was David.

Will took a deep breath, put the radio up to his mouth, and pressed the button.

"We're here, over."

CHAPTER SIXTEEN
GABRIEL

The heavy duffle bag hanging from his side swung and hit Gabriel in his right thigh with every stride as he rounded the corner at the end of the row of stores. When he made it to the parking lot in the front of the mall, he saw that it now consisted primarily of empty vehicles. The loitering dead were now behind him, completing their circle around the back of the buildings after following him into the sporting goods store.

As he ran, the place where the boy was supposed to be standing came into view, but Dylan wasn't there.

Gabriel arrived at the spot at the edge of the woods and looked side to side, scanning for the boy.

"Dylan!" he called out.

No response.

"Dylan!" Gabriel cried out again, his voice shaking.

He looked back to see the horde, a couple hundred yards away, coming around the corner at the back of the shopping center.

Then he heard a faint sniffle and cry.

Gabriel ran into the woods, following the sound of a child in fear. He didn't have to run far before he came across Dylan, sitting on the ground in front of a tree, his face buried into his arms. In front of him, a body lay on its back with ghostly eyes and pale, faded skin. It had a hole in its forehead, seeping with blood.

Gabriel approached the boy and knelt down. He reached out to comfort him.

"Dylan, it's Gab..."

The boy panicked, waving his arms and bringing the pistol up in front of his face. Gabriel reacted before Dylan pulled the trigger and the bullet went just over his shoulder.

"Whoa," Gabriel said, reaching out and snatching the gun from the boy's grasp.

Dylan broke out into tears, jumped to his feet, and embraced Gabriel's neck.

"I'm so sorry. I had to. I had to kill him," Dylan said.

Gabriel ran his hand up and down the boy's back, sending autumn leaves back to the forest floor.

"It's okay," Gabriel said. He put his hands on the boy's shoulder and pushed him away to where he could look him in the eyes. "Why didn't you run back to the plane like I asked?"

Dylan wiped his eyes and shook his head. Sniffling, he said, "I couldn't. My legs locked up and I fell down right here. He lunged at me and I had no choice."

Gabriel rubbed the boy's head, running his fingers through his hair as he would to comfort his own child.

Behind them, they heard the faint howls of the approaching herd.

He put his hands on Dylan's cold cheeks. "Can you move your legs now?"

Dylan nodded.

"Good. Come on..."

***

The sun was completely hidden, leaving Gabriel and Dylan in the dark among the dead. They came out of the trees and heard the horde to their left, getting closer. For a moment, they came to a stop while Gabriel thought of their next move. Most of the tall light posts in the parking lot still worked, powering up at their usual, automated time. Gabriel used the light to scan the parking lot and, to his right at the edge of the lot, he saw a large SUV.

"Come on," Gabriel told Dylan, and they ran away from the horde, towards the SUV.

The door on the truck had been left open by the driver, but no body was in sight. Gabriel opened the back door and threw the two bags and the rifle onto the back seat. He looked to Dylan.

"Get in the back."

The boy did as he was told, using the step on the side of the truck to elevate himself onto the leather back seat.

Gabriel jumped into the driver's seat and checked the ignition for keys that weren't there. Then, like every movie he had ever seen, he checked under the sun visor and in the glove compartment for a spare. Nothing.

"Hurry! They're coming!" Dylan yelled.

And he was right. The congregation of the dead was limping their way closer and closer to the truck, gathered like the runners of a marathon.

Before Gabriel shut the glove box, he felt something made of steel and pulled it out. He smiled as he clicked on the flashlight with a turn of the head, realizing the mistake he'd made in not picking one up while in the sporting goods store.

He considered himself lucky for having found one and handed the light back to Dylan.

"I need you to lean up here and shine this light under the steering wheel. And I need you to hold it steady. Can you do that for me?"

Dylan nodded.

Gabriel got out of the truck and knelt down, reaching under the wheel and busting open a compartment full of wiring.

"Do you know what you are doing?" Dylan asked.

"Yeah, sure," Gabriel lied. Jimmy, his brother-in-law, who'd taught him how to shoot, had shown him how to hot wire a car once, just because he knew how to do it and wanted to brag about it to his visiting in-laws. It was the last thing Gabriel ever thought he would have been thankful for, until now.

Now, Gabriel split the wires and began to run them together, trying to create a spark that would start the truck. Nothing happened.

"Hurry," Dylan shouted.

The undead were only about fifty yards away now, using their cannibalistic sense to follow the trail of the man and the boy.

"Fuck! Come on," Gabriel mumbled to himself.

He ran the copper innards of two of the wires together and heard a bolt. A small spark came off the wires and he heard the motor begin to rumble.

"Come on!"

The engine turned over.

"Yes!" Gabriel shouted.

He looked up and saw a wide-eyed Dylan pointing behind him.

"Look out!"

Gabriel turned and saw it lunging at him. It was his instinct that pulled the knife from its sheath and thrusted it up through the creature's throat and through its head. The others had almost reached the truck, and Gabriel withdrew the knife, turned, and jumped into the driver's seat before slamming the door behind him.

He threw the column shift into *Drive* and floored the gas pedal, sending the tires into a wailing screech, leaving the horde aimlessly reaching at them from their left as they sped away down one of the lanes of the parking lot.

***

Five minutes later, on the open road, Gabriel pulled the truck over onto the shoulder. Every car they passed was abandoned. Either most of the population had turned, or Gabriel was the only person dumb enough to be driving around at night while the beasts lurked in the streets.

Gabriel shut off the lights so they wouldn't gather any attention, and looked back at Dylan.

"You okay?"

Dylan nodded. "I'm hungry. Did you find me something to eat?"

Gabriel shook his head.

The boy sighed, looking down to his hands as they moved to his stomach. Gabriel's own stomach screamed at him, but nothing hurt him more than seeing the scared, innocent child aching with hunger.

Gabriel looked down and noticed a bottle of water three-quarters full in one of the cup holders. His first instinct was to grab it and squeeze the plastic bottle dry. But the boy needed it more than he did. He took the bottle and handed it back to Dylan.

"Drink this," he said. "We can't get food right now, but you need to at least drink some water."

Dylan accepted the bottle, smacking his dry lips. He unscrewed the cap, tossed it to the side, and began to drink the water as fast as he could, squeezing the plastic bottle in his small hand. Because of the mild temperature outside, the water was still cool, and comforted his throat on the way down.

When more than half of the contents was gone, Dylan looked to Gabriel, who was watching him.

"Drink up," Gabriel said.

Dylan looked at the bottle and then extended his arm, offering the rest of the water to Gabriel.

Gabriel shook his head. "You drink it."

"I'm fine. You need to have some, too," Dylan replied.

A smile grew on Gabriel's face. He accepted the water, pressing the mouth of the bottle to his lips, and feeling the water wet his tongue and slide down his throat, which had a slight sting in it from the shock of hydration. He gasped as he took the last drop of water from the bottle and looked to Dylan.

"Thank you," he said.

Dylan smiled. He turned the cab light on above them, and reached for the bags.

"What's in here?" the boy asked.

Gabriel reached back between the front seats and

grabbed Dylan's arm.

"Whoa, whoa. Hold on there, champ."

Ducking his head, Gabriel crawled between the front seats and joined Dylan in the backseat. He opened the bags and pulled out the clothes he'd gotten for Dylan.

"Hope these fit."

Dylan's eyes lit up like he'd woken up on Christmas morning and seen the bike he had been asking Santa about for months. The clothes on his back were sticking to him from all the sweat and dirt, and he was beyond thankful for the new digs. He gave Gabriel a hug.

"Thank you."

Gabriel smiled. He was happy to see at least a little joy in Dylan's face, imagining that the boy had to be missing his parents dearly. It made him think of Sarah. She was likely missing him just as much as he missed her. He wanted to think that his wife and daughter were alive, so, in his mind, he *knew* they were.

"We should try the radio," Dylan said.

It was a great idea, one that Gabriel should have thought of sooner, but his mind had been so focused on getting the boy away from danger.

Gabriel leaned into the front seat and pushed the volume knob, feeling the click on the tip of his finger as the radio powered on.

Static buzzed through the speakers as Gabriel pressed the *Seek* button.

The radio found a signal and stopped on 94.7.

"Turn it up," Dylan said.

Gabriel turned the knob.

This is the Emergency Broadcast System with an urgent message. The state of Tennessee has issued a house arrest for all residents until further notice. Please be advised that no one is allowed outside until the ban is lifted. Failure to abide by these laws will result in instant prosecution. Again, do not leave your home.

This is the Emergency Broadcast...

Gabriel shut off the radio.

"What are we gonna do?" Dylan asked. "I've never been arrested."

The innocence made Gabriel smile, an emotion he needed to feel after hearing the warning from the radio.

"Well, I haven't seen any police, have you?"

Dylan shook his head.

Gabriel wedged back into the front seat and reclined the chair, resting the back of his head against it.

"Let's get some rest," Gabriel said. "We'll have to wait and find food in the morning when there's light."

***

The following morning, Gabriel was awoken by a noise so distant that he was surprised it roused him. He slowly sat up in the front seat and saw the oncoming car speeding down the road.

His eyes widened.

People.

Gabriel hurried to open the door and stepped out of the truck. He stood next to the hood, waving his arms frantically in the air.

In the back seat, Dylan began to wake and rose his head

to see the oncoming car. He was too tired to be as interested in it, his tender mind not able to process what this could mean so soon after waking.

The car wasn't slowing down.

"Hey! Hey!" Gabriel screamed, jumping up and down now while continuing to flail his hands.

When the car came within fifty yards, Gabriel realized the driver wasn't going to slow down. He dived into the driver's seat of the SUV, pulling the door shut just before the speeding car would have taken it off its hinges.

"Why didn't they stop?" Dylan asked.

Gabriel just leaned down and ran the two wires together, starting the truck.

"Put on your seatbelt," he told Dylan. "Now."

The engine turned over and Gabriel turned the wheel all the way to the left, and punched the gas flush against the floorboard, the tail of the white car a small blur in the distance.

CHAPTER SEVENTEEN
WILL

"Are you able to pinpoint your exact location in this building?" Will asked Marcus over the radio. He and Holly were still standing in the office at the front part of the facility.

"The lights went out before we got back to this part of the building," Marcus began. "All I know is that I was struggling with a couple of these things, I felt a door, and I opened it. The room is solid concrete and there are no windows. It's some kind of storage vault or something. There is no way these things are gonna get in, but I hear them outside. Luckily, the roof of the room isn't concrete, so I can actually get a radio signal through."

Will rolled his eyes, not particularly caring for the extra information. He just wanted to know where Marcus was so that they could extract him and get out of here.

"Do you know how many of them are back there?" Will asked.

"At least fifteen," Marcus said. "Enough to make me about go crazy back here."

Will and Holly could hear the hissing and scratching through the radio while Marcus talked.

"Alright. We are going to try and come get you. Do not radio us again unless it's an emergency. We don't want them to hear us. If we get to a safe spot, we will call you and check in," Will told him.

"Alright. Please hurry."

Will rolled his eyes again and looked over to Holly.

"You ready for this?"

Holly nodded. "I'm ready. I won't freeze again, I promise."

Will took a few steps toward the door that led to the warehouse. He took the flashlight in his hand and stuck it under his arm that held the gun, putting his now free hand on the door knob.

"Let's do this."

***

Like the facility Will had spent the last two days in, the warehouse was in pitch black darkness, only this building didn't have a crack in the roof to bring in at least some sunlight the way the warehouse at Element had.

Will stepped through the door first, the little bit of light peeking through the door from the office windows allowing him to see to his immediate left and right that it was clear. He looked back to Holly and cocked his head, signaling her to follow him.

They could see the outlines of the large metal racking in the warehouse. In the distance, the baying of the hounds, but no Empties seemed to be near them. Will pulled out the flashlight and clicked it on.

There were boxes all over the ground. If he hadn't turned on the flashlight, one of them would have fallen for sure, likely attracting Empties.

"It sounds like they might all be in the back," Will

whispered. "Near the room he's trapped in. We need to figure out the best way to get back there."

Holly licked her lips, the smack cutting through the silent air, and said, "Maybe if we go to the last aisle, and then walk to the back from there, we can sneak around and they won't see us. I know the layout of this place a little bit. We should have a straight shot back there."

Will nodded his head, agreeing.

They began their walk to the last aisle of the warehouse, stepping slowly so as not to make a lot of noise and attract any of the Empties. Will scanned the area in front of them with the flashlight, giving bits of hope in the utter darkness.

Holly tripped, barely keeping herself upright and somehow holding in a scream. She let out a small yelp, but nothing loud enough to attract any of the horde.

But when Will turned around and flashed the light on the ground where she had stumbled, it was much harder for Holly to hold in her emotion.

He quickly shuffled over and covered her mouth, as the light moved away from the decaying body on the floor. Even though he had grown immune to seeing it, a body showing up in the beam of his flashlight had startled him.

Holly turned away, burying her head into his shoulders. Will took the flashlight and pointed it down at the body. The head was completely detached, sitting next to the shoulder, lying flat on one of the cheeks. The face was battered and torn, and the flesh from the upper body had been skinned and eaten. From the hairstyle, he assumed that it was a man. There wasn't much evidence left to prove otherwise.

"We gotta keep moving," Will told Holly.

She moved away from him and they continued making their way to the last aisle.

When they reached a wall, Will instinctively turned to the right and saw four Empties on the ground, gathered around something. The flashlight grabbed their attention, and they snarled as they began toward Will and Holly.

Holly turned to run but Will stopped her, grabbing her shoulder.

"There's nowhere to go. We have to take them out," he said.

"But it will attract the others. And we aren't even sure how many there are yet," she replied.

Will shrugged. "Doesn't matter. We gotta hold our ground."

He handed her the flashlight.

"Shine this on them so I can see them. Just give me light and cover me."

Holly stood behind Will, aiming the light at the first of the four. He turned and put the rifle to his shoulder, taking aim at the Empty directly in front of him.

The shot rang off the walls and the solid floors, sending an echo through the 40,000-square-foot concrete warehouse. The Empty body dropped to the ground, and they heard howls coming from the back of the warehouse. They couldn't be sure how many, but it sounded like a large group.

Holly froze and the light didn't move.

Will turned to her.

"Holly, I need light," he yelled.

She shook her head and snapped out of her trance,

moving the light to the next, and then the next.

Only missing twice, Will finished taking out the small group.

Holly flashed the light to where the Empties had stood and saw what she thought were the remains of a stray cat, torn to pieces by the dead.

She turned and threw up on the concrete floor. Will grabbed the flashlight from her hand and shined it down the end of the aisle, hearing the growls get closer.

The light shone on the eyes of at least eight Empties, coming at them with outstretched arms and open jaws.

Their noises sounded as if they were surrounding them, and he turned the light to his right to see another group coming at them.

"Shit!" Will said.

He grabbed Holly under the arm, turned, and ran down the other end of the aisle toward the front of the warehouse.

It was a dead end.

CHAPTER EIGHTEEN
JESSICA

It was a frail shriek. One that echoed through the house and represented the crumbling heart of a broken woman. A young woman burdened with seeing what lay in front of her.

Melissa turned from the front door and ran up the stairs. She took the right at the top and saw Jessica on her knees, weeping at the head of her parents' bed.

Her parents.

Matt and Alexandra "Alex" Davies lay motionless on the bed. From where she stood, Melissa couldn't see why, but she did see the matching red stains that flowed up the headboard and onto the wall. Above their bed was a black and white painting of a forest, and the dried blood added a dark element to the piece.

Melissa moved closer before having to cover her mouth and turn away.

The Davies' each held a pistol in one of their hands while their other hands remained clasped together.

Matt and Alex Davies had committed suicide, lying together in their most intimate and vulnerable place.

Jessica wept, crying on the floor and utterly confused. Why had her parents taken their own lives? There were no sick people in front of the house threatening them. The house itself was untouched. Had they just given up?

The thought angered Jessica. How could her parents just give up? She stood up and began to scream, pulling her hair and shaking her head. Jessica looked at the dresser to her left and ran her hands down it, throwing all the photographs, jewelry, and miscellaneous stuff onto the floor. She turned the dresser over, watching the mirror fall to the ground and shatter. A flat screen television was mounted to the wall behind her and Jessica tore it off its mount, watching it suffer the same fate as the mirror, as electronic pieces scattered everywhere.

Melissa looked away from the couple on the bed, her hands covering her mouth as she cried.

When Jessica stopped wrecking the room, she went back down to her knees and lay her head on the edge of the bed, gripping the sheets and pulling them to her, biting down on the edge of them.

Melissa heard a crash and ran to the top of the stairs. She looked down and saw a hand coming through the door. She ran back into the room and put her hands on Jessica's shoulders.

"Sweetie, we gotta go."

"No," Jessica yelled.

Sweat began to trickle off Melissa's brow.

"We can't stay here. That thing is almost in the house." More banging. "And it may not be alone."

Jessica kept her face on the bed.

"Just leave me here. Let me just give up and die here like them."

A stern look came across Melissa's face. She put her hands on Jessica's chin and forced her to look at her.

"You're not gonna do that to me, you hear me? You didn't give up on me when I lost the love of my life and I am damn sure not going to give up on you. There's still a life for us out there. And my son is out there. I need you, Jessica."

Jessica looked at her parents. The intrusion downstairs continued.

"Please," Melissa said.

Two beasts fought their way into the house.

While they were lucky that Ross Street had been mostly void of the dead, Jessica and Melissa knew that attention would be drawn to the home now.

The creatures stared up the stairs at the two women and howled. Jessica waited for the first one to make it halfway up the stairs before drawing the pistol and taking two shots to hit it in the head. The beast, a man in its previous life, fell back and sent its formally woman companion tumbling down the stairs. Jessica and Melissa hurried down to the bottom level, Jessica stopping to put a bullet through the head of the female, pinned under the male creature and flailing her arms everywhere. The gun sang and the arms fell.

Before running to the door, Jessica ran into the living room and grabbed a family photo sitting on the coffee table, as well as the picture of her and her mom off the wall, the one that Melissa had seen earlier.

"They are coming," Melissa called.

Jessica ran to the door and took one last look back into her childhood house. It wouldn't sink in until later that she would never be back here. But she wiped her eyes and ran to the van.

***

Melissa sat in the driver's seat, waving Jessica into the van. The sliding side door was open and Jessica jumped in. The van was moving before she was able to slide the door shut or put her seat belt on, and the sharp turn out of the yard that Melissa made almost slung Jessica out of the vehicle. She held on and managed to shut the door, securing herself with the seatbelt once the van straightened.

More beasts had gathered on Ross Street and the two women knew that they were lucky to get out of the house when they did. The undead were walking over from the main street of the neighborhood, and blocked the entire side of the street that they had arrived from.

Jessica pointed to her right. "Go that way. There's a back entrance out of the neighborhood."

Melissa nodded and followed Jessica's direction, moving away from the horde of the undead. They reached the back of the neighborhood with little resistance, and Melissa headed left down a back road.

"About a quarter mile ahead, you can take a left and you'll see signs for the interstate."

Melissa tapped the brakes as they approached the turn and moved the wheel counterclockwise. She saw the sign for the interstate and veered to the right to take the ramp.

Jessica put her head back against the seat. Like Melissa with Walt, she was allowed no time to mourn. The two women had experienced loss in similar but different forms, both extreme.

Melissa turned around and looked at Jessica.

"Are you okay, honey?"

As she was turned around, a deer ran in front of the van.

"Look out!" Jessica screamed, pointing to the deer.

Eyes wide, Melissa swerved hard to the right. The van lost control and began to roll. Jessica tensed and tried to hold on to the seat in front of her, but it was useless. The van flipped three times before coming to a stop right side up.

Jessica shook her head as the van ceased to roll. Instantly, her head hurt and her neck felt like a piece of gum. She put her head into her palm and felt the warm blood before the scent of iron hit her nose.

Her vision came back and she saw Melissa slumped over, her face in the air bag; she wasn't moving.

When Jessica tried to free herself to help her, the pain hit like a fire in her shoulder. Her collarbone was broken.

Behind her, she heard a rumbling coming toward them. She looked in the rearview mirror and saw through the cracked window a white vehicle approaching them.

"Oh shit," she said. If her only experience with the living, since everything had changed, was any sign of things to come, they were in trouble.

"Melissa," she yelled out to no response.

The engine stopped next to their van as Jessica stirred, trying to come up with an idea of how to get out.

Multiple gunshots rang through the air. Jessica jumped, feeling the pain in her shoulder as her body jolted.

She looked out the window and saw the vehicle. It was an ambulance.

The passenger side door of the ambulance opened and she watched a well-built, dark man, pull a gun up to chin height and unload a clip into one of the beasts.

Their eyes met. He ran over to the van and looked

through the window at her.

"We gotta get y'all out of there," the EMT said. "Open up!"

***

Jessica sat up, disoriented, with little sense of where she was. Pain hit her shoulder immediately and she grimaced. A hand touched her good shoulder, giving it a slight push.

"Lie back, miss. You're going to be alright."

She blinked a few times and looked up to see the man who had pulled her out of the van.

"Where am I?"

The man checked her heartbeat with a stethoscope, found that her beats were getting back to normal, and wrapped it around his neck.

"You're in an ambulance. The wreck was really bad. Your collarbone is broken and you likely suffered a concussion."

Jessica looked around the ambulance and tried to sit up again.

"Whoa," the EMT said. "Just relax."

"Where is Melissa?"

He put his hand up, palm out, urging her to calm down.

"She's fine. We called in a second ambulance to come get her. She was worse off than you. Knocked out. But she's going to be fine."

Jessica put her hand to her forehead, feeling her head wound for the first time. Raising her left arm wasn't easy, but her right arm, which had slammed against the door and broken her collarbone, wouldn't move up at all.

"My name is Lawrence. What's yours?"

"Jessica."

156

He smiled. "Nice to meet you, Jessica. Sorry it's under this circumstance."

Jessica couldn't even crack a small smile, but she gave Lawrence a nod. He was attractive, and she wanted to smile, but in this moment of pain, loss, and grief, she couldn't muster it up. Not even for the man who'd saved her, the second stranger in two days to complete the task.

A small bag sat on a flat surface near her and she saw the photographs she'd taken from her parents' house poking out of the top of it. She closed her eyes, letting out a sigh of relief that the memories weren't lost.

"Do you know what happened?" Jessica asked.

Lawrence filled his cheeks and let out a large breath. "Melissa, right? She must have swerved..."

Jessica cut him off. "I mean with the people outside."

Lawrence frowned and shook his head. "We have some theories, but we aren't sure. Watching them all fall down, it's something I just can't even begin to try and understand."

Jessica squinted. "Fall down?"

He glared at her. "Where were you when it happened?"

Jessica thought back to the moment when the elevator door opened and she'd seen the frightened people on the 8th floor of the hotel.

"I wasn't around any people," she said, remembering the time lapse between leaving the front desk, going down to housekeeping and dry storage where she was alone, and then up to the rooms where she first saw the people who were sick.

Lawrence took a deep breath and crossed his arms over his knees, using his tongue to wet his lips so that he could speak clearly.

"I was out on an emergency call. My partner and I were called over to a recreational park where a man had had a heart attack while playing softball. Guess the guy was past his prime.

"I was performing mouth-to-mouth on the man when I heard a collective gasp. My partner, Robin, was down. I shook her, checked her for a pulse, and found that she wasn't breathing. Chest compressions did nothing for her.

"When I looked around, I saw that most of the people in the park had fallen. Everyone who didn't fall just stood there, confused and frightened.

"Then, moments later, it happened."

"The bodies rose?" Jessica said.

Lawrence nodded.

"I was lucky. I was distracted, in utter shock of everything, as I watched people begin to eat people. Then, Robin grabbed me. I honestly don't remember how I got away, but I did."

"Oh my God!" Jessica said.

Lawrence laughed. "Something tells me He was involved."

Jessica cocked her head. "God?"

Lawrence shrugged. "That's my theory at least. I believe in the book of Revelation. And I think we witnessed the Rapture. Only, while the Bible describes people disappearing, I think only their souls disappeared. And that thing we see left is nothing but a vacant shell."

Jessica only listened, didn't respond. Her faith had always been shaky at best, and the past 48 hours hadn't done much to help it.

"Anyways, I was able to get a small group of survivors into the ambulance and head back to the hospital. That's where we're headed."

"Is it safe?"

Lawrence nodded. "We were able to quarantine ourselves in the west wing of the building. We aren't strong in numbers, but we have power, supplies, food. You'll be taken care of there."

Jessica lay her head down and let out a sigh.

Turning away from Jessica, Lawrence began to put together a syringe. He loaded it and flicked it twice, making sure the medicine was set.

"We will be there soon, but I want to give you an anesthetic. You need to sleep and you won't be able to through the pain. This should put you out enough where we can work on you once we get there, in just a few minutes. This isn't our normal procedure, but I don't think that much matters anymore."

Jessica smiled.

"Thank you," she told him.

Lawrence smiled back. "Just relax."

He found a vein in her arm and injected the anesthetic into it.

Within moments, the roof of the van became cloudy. Jessica's head fell over and the last thing she saw before she fell asleep was the picture of her parents' smiling faces, hanging out of the bag.

CHAPTER NINETEEN
WILL

When they reached the front of the aisle, Will realized the racking extended all the way to the wall, trapping them. He flashed the light at the racks and saw that each rack was filled with pallets of large, metal blocks.

He tried to move one of the pallets so that they could duck through the racks, but it didn't budge.

The Empties, now in a group of nearly twenty, inched closer by the moment.

"What are we gonna do?" Holly cried.

Will looked up. He threw the gun around to his back and looked over to Holly.

"Shine the light up there."

Holly pointed the light at the racks and Will climbed five feet to the second level, standing on the orange beam and using the objects on the pallet next to him for balance.

"Come on!" he yelled down, reaching his hand down to help her up.

She grabbed his hand and Will pulled her up to the second level of the racking. Holly flashed the light down to see the Empties only yards away.

"We have to get higher," Will said.

He reached up and grabbed the beam above his head, pulling himself up, thankful for the pull-up bar under his bathroom door at home. One of the pallets at the top was empty, and Will spread across it on his belly, extending his arms down to Holly.

When she reached up, she slipped on one of the slick metal beams.

Will reached down and caught the arm of the screaming girl just as she was about to fall. He had a tight hold on her forearms and worked to pull her up, grimacing as his biceps bulged through his shirt.

Below her, one of the Empties screamed back at her, grabbing her legs.

She began to panic, kicking her legs as she felt the slimy dead hands wrap around her ankles.

"I've got you!" Will yelled. "Hang on!"

It began to dig its worn nails into her calf as it scratched and pulled. Holly let out a scream that echoed through the facility, tears rolling down her face.

Will grunted as he pulled, fighting the surprising strength of the creature below. Her frantic kicking wasn't making things any easier, either.

Rapid shots rang through the air as Empties at the back of the pack began to fall. Will could only see black outlines disappear, and he heard each let out a grizzly yell as they hit the concrete.

The Empty let go of Holly's leg and Will finally pulled her up to the top level.

The gunshots of a semi-automatic weapon continued to scream off the walls.

Will pointed the light down to the ground and saw the creature that had a grip on Holly fall to the ground, losing its head in the process.

Once he knew that Holly was secure, Will panned the light across the ground, seeing the collection of dead bodies stacked in rows on the ground.

Will shined the light a little further on and saw a black man carrying an assault rifle and looking up at them.

Holly squinted her eyes.

"Marcus?"

The man nodded and let out an echoing laugh.

***

The three of them moved back into the office part of the building where there was light.

With a smile across his face and the assault rifle over his shoulder, Marcus followed Will and Holly through the door into the office. He wore a neatly kempt mustache on his face and had matching hair on his chin, though they didn't connect. His eyes were as bright as his smile, but his scent was dull and reeked of his reality—several hours trapped in a small room.

Marcus gave Holly a hug, letting his chin rest on her shoulder. "It's good to see you, Ms. McNeil."

"Likewise," she said back.

They broke their embrace and Marcus looked over to Will, extending his hand to him.

"Thanks," Marcus said.

Will chuckled as he accepted the hand. "I should be thanking you."

Marcus shook his head. "Nah, man. You all distracted them long enough for me to get out of there. Once I heard the gunshots, I put my ear to the door. The scratching and awful scream of those things stopped pretty quick after the shots. I counted to a hundred then got out of the room and came to find y'all."

"Well, thanks, regardless," Will said.

Marcus nodded. He looked over to Holly. "How is everyone else?"

She bowed her head and didn't respond.

"They'd be doing a lot better if that asshole wasn't over there holding a leash on everyone," Will chimed in.

"What?" Marcus asked.

"That asshole, David Ellis," Will said with a smile.

Marcus approached Will, glaring at him the entire time he moved closer. He stood about a foot away from Will now.

"You ever think that maybe *you're* the asshole?" Marcus asked.

Will scoffed and said, "Yeah. The asshole who just saved your shit 'cause that pussy didn't wanna come do it."

Marcus threw Will against the wall and pressed his forearm against Will's throat, pinning him against the drywall.

"I don't know who the fuck you are, man, but I'm not gonna let you talk about my friend like that, okay? David is a good man," Marcus said.

Will was hardly able to get a small chuckle out through the arm on his throat. "Yeah? Well, if that prick is your idea of a friend, maybe I should have just let those things tear your ass apart."

Anger spread across Marcus' face and he sent a soaring left through the air and connected with the right side of Will's face, just below his eye.

"Marcus! Marcus, stop!" Holly yelled.

He turned and looked at her.

"He's right, Marcus," she said. "It's not the same. *He* isn't the same."

"What do you mean?" Marcus asked.

She began to sob, lightly. "He's over there trying to control everyone. Tell everyone what to do."

"He's the boss," Marcus said.

She shook her head. "No, Marcus. This is different. He's acting like some kind of dictator or mayor or something. Like he's trying to start a new community within that fucking building and make himself the king. Besides, you think he's still our boss?"

Holly went to the window and pulled the blinds down.

"Look outside, Marcus," she continued. "You think that job titles really fucking matter now?"

Marcus looked at her, his eyes slanted and stern. Then, he looked away with pouty lips as he tried to digest everything she was saying.

She had begun to tear up, not convinced she was getting through to him.

"For Christ's sake, Marcus. He pulled a gun on me."

His head turned quickly toward her right as the radio on his belt began to buzz.

"Anyone there? Over," David Ellis said through the walkie.

Not letting his eyes leave Holly and keeping Will pinned against the wall, Marcus slowly reached for the radio and pressed the button with his worn thumb.

"David. It's Marcus. I'm out. Over."

***

Will reached up, grabbing onto Jonas' forearm and pulling himself up into the warehouse while the Empties remained distracted behind him by the road flare in the parking lot, the flare still spraying red sparks and smoke into the sky.

He looked over to see David and Marcus embracing, as if they hadn't seen each other since high school. Holly had taken a seat to Will's left, still trying to allow her nerves to recover from all she had seen and experienced during the impromptu rescue mission.

Jonas reached out his hand to Will and waved his fingers toward himself.

"I don't think you'll be needing that anymore," Jonas said, looking at the gun.

Will looked at the rifle, reluctant to give it back. He had no trust for the people around him and hated the situation he was in, but knew that he was probably left with little choice but to hand the weapon over. He wasn't going to start firing at everyone—he'd be dead within seconds—so he let the strap of the rifle slide off his shoulder and he handed it to Jonas.

Removing his hand from Marcus' shoulder, David walked over to Will, smiling. He reached his hand out, offering it to Will in a kind of thank you or truce.

Will stood there for a moment, unsure what to do or think. He had no trust for this man. In fact, he hated him. A kind of hate that his humble blood had never felt for anyone else.

Reluctantly, he put his hand out and grasped David's.

"Thank you," David said.

Will nodded.

As Will loosened the grip of the handshake, David tightened it suddenly, pulling Will toward him and slamming his left fist into Will's stomach as hard as he could.

Will let out a grunt and leaned over, gripping the pain in his stomach.

David brought his knee up across Will's face, sending him to the ground. Will could barely move. He rolled on the ground, holding his stomach and writhing.

The crowd behind David began to rustle. Holly jumped out of her chair, screaming, and ran toward Will.

"Get her!" David commanded two of the other men in the room.

They came over and picked Holly up under her arms, moving her away from Will.

David leaned down and turned Will over at the edge of the dock, digging his knee into the middle of Will's back with all his weight.

"What are you doing, David?" Marcus asked, walking toward him.

Jonas stepped in front of Marcus, shaking his head from side to side.

Marcus stepped back, looking down to the gun pointed at his stomach. He looked back up and glared at Jonas, a look of disgust in his eyes.

David used his strength to slide Will's body across the smooth concrete of the warehouse floor, leaving Will's head hanging over the edge of the dock, exposed to the world.

Holly kept screaming uncontrollably, piercing the air.

David rolled his eyes and turned around. "Take her inside!"

The two men carried Holly into another part of the building, her screams becoming a faint, white noise.

David grabbed Will's head up by his hair. One of his eyes was nearly swollen shut, but Will could see the group of Empties only twenty yards away, still distracted by the flare. David leaned down into Will's ear.

"You are strong, son," David whispered. "Too strong. You must understand that I can't have a threat to my control hanging around here, can't you? We have to do away with that."

"Fuck you," Will said, spitting blood onto the asphalt below.

David pulled back harder on Will's hair, making him groan.

"No. Fuck you, kid," David replied.

David whistled.

Three of the Empties turned, spitting toward the dock. This caught the attention of the others, and they began limping toward the building.

Will tried to fight it, his head hanging over the edge—exposed—only six feet above the ground. He wiggled his body back and forth as David dug his knee harder into his back.

"David, don't do this!" Marcus pleaded, Jonas still disrupting his path. "He saved me!"

"Yes, but he plans to kill me!" David said.

"Let's just let him go!" Marcus said.

The Empties were limping closer.

"It's not that easy, Marcus. This isn't the same world. We have to do what we have to do to survive. Who's to say, if I let him go, that he won't just come back here and seek revenge on me for tying him up and forcing him to go get you?"

Closer. Dead arms beginning to extend.

"Yeah," Marcus replied. "And I wouldn't be here if it wasn't for him." Hurt crept into his voice. "Let him go, David."

The Empties were close. The first one could almost reach out and touch Will.

David licked his lips and grimaced, taking a tighter grip on Will's hair.

He bit his lip and pulled back on Will, right before the baying creature could grab him.

Will rolled over and coughed, unable to catch his breath and in shock from his near demise.

David stood. He looked over to Marcus, running his hands together, holding the glare on him.

"Lock this piece of shit up," David told Jonas, pointing down at Will.

***

The large man led Will into a small room, shutting the door behind him.

David watched the door close and then retreated to his office.

Marcus stood in the middle of the warehouse, looking out of the large bay door at the Empties. At the very left edge of his view, he saw a white car appear, moving down the hill that led into the industrial park.

"They're back!" Leon yelled from the loading dock. Along

with Jonas, he was David's other primary member of security. He pulled a radio from his belt and repeated the same message to someone on the other end.

On the side of the building, there was an area twenty feet wide that extended all the way to the rear of the building, surrounded by an eight-foot tall chain link fence. Marcus walked to the edge of the dock and watched the white car pull up to the fence to his left. He jumped as Leon lit a road flare and threw it out into the parking lot to his right. The Empties howled and followed the flare.

"All clear," Leon said into the radio.

Marcus heard a rumble and watched as the fence began to open, allowing the vehicle to drive through to safety.

"And that's that," Leon said, smiling at Marcus.

Marcus looked across the warehouse to the yellow door that led into David's office. He could see him sitting at his desk with one hand to his chin and his other scribbling notes on a piece of paper. Marcus strode to the room and barged through the closed door.

David looked up from his notes to Marcus, laying his palms flat on the desk.

"What the hell are you doing, David?" Marcus asked.

David shook his head, smiling, and looked back down at his papers.

Marcus brought his fist down onto the desk, knocking over a cup full of pens.

"Answer me!"

Jonas, back from tying up Will, approached the window with Leon. David looked up and waved them off, signaling to them that everything was okay.

David sighed and put his palm up, pointing toward the chair at the front of his desk.

"Have a seat, Marcus."

The chair in front of him was a standard wooden office guest chair with an ugly blue cushion. Marcus pulled the back of the chair and sat down, never letting his eyes leave David's.

David licked his lips, supported himself on the desk with his elbows, and leaned toward Marcus.

"You have to understand something, Marcus," he began. "I have nothing but the best intentions for all of you. You realize that, right?"

Marcus nodded. "Yeah, but..."

David cut him off, holding his index finger into the air.

"Rich and Mike have made multiple trips out there. And the news they have brought back hasn't been pretty." David grabbed his coffee mug and took a sip, the steam rising in front of his face. "The world has changed, Marcus. And we have to change with it."

Marcus shrugged and shook his head. "Okay, but what does any of this have to do with holding that innocent guy hostage in there?"

David clasped his hands together. He looked out the window of his office and saw the people, *his* people, each in their assigned position, doing as he asked. The power brought a certain tingle through him; it was almost an erotic, arousing sensation.

"He's a threat, Marcus."

Marcus squinted his face. "To what? Your little kingdom here?"

David leaned back. "You'll see, Marcus. Just be patient, friend."

The eyes of Marcus' friend had changed. He saw it now, just like Holly had warned him in the building next door. He slowly rose from his chair, pushing it back under the desk.

"Okay," Marcus said softly.

Hands in his pockets, he turned and headed for the door, knowing that *those* eyes stared into the center of his back the entire time.

Before he made his exit, Marcus turned back to David and asked him one more question.

"Did you put a gun to Holly's head?"

For a moment, David remained quiet. He ran his fingers over the stubble on his chin as he tried to read the reasoning behind Marcus' question by looking into his eyes.

"Whatever it takes," David said as he looked back down to what he was writing.

Marcus shook his head and exited the room.

CHAPTER TWENTY
GABRIEL

"Dylan, just sit back!" Gabriel commanded.

The boy kept leaning into the front seat, distracting Gabriel, who was trying to keep the white car in his sights.

They were speeding past old vacant businesses in a poor part of town. There were abandoned gas stations, coffee shops, and boutiques lining the road. It appeared that most of the people who survived were following the house arrest brought down by the government. Everyone except the person in the white car.

In the distance, he saw the car veer off onto the entry ramp of a highway.

Gabriel exited onto the ramp when he reached it. He saw the car climbing a hill in the horizon.

When the car disappeared over the hill, he finally lost it. Gabriel drove over the hill, but never saw the car.

"Shit!" he yelled, banging his hands on the steering wheel.

He came to a stop on the shoulder, realizing he wasn't sure where he was. Nashville was unfamiliar to him, and he had been so focused on the car in the distance that he wasn't paying attention to where he was going. He only knew that he was on a highway. Like everywhere else, many cars had been left abandoned. There were a few undead drifters in the distance, far enough away to where they were of no threat to him and Dylan.

Dylan moved into the front seat. As he did, he saw something in the distance.

"What is that?" Dylan asked. He was pointing the same way the truck was headed.

Smoke rose on the horizon, not far from where the truck sat. Gabriel threw the shifter into *Drive* and pressed the gas with his toes.

A couple of miles down the road, he reached an exit that looked like it led to the smoke. He veered the truck to the right and took the ramp, dodging abandoned cars and more of the undead.

At the end of the ramp, he took another right and let the car creep down the street, his foot barely touching the gas pedal.

Gabriel's eyes widened as he looked down and saw two black tire marks on the street in front of him. They looked fresh and he could smell the burnt rubber in the air. He let the car settle at the top of the road. On the corner, there was a sign that read *Space Park East - Industrial Park*. Gabriel saw that the road went for about half a mile with small buildings on either side before it hit a curve. The smoke rose still, further east from where they parked, but Gabriel could sense there was life down this street.

He pressed down on the gas and followed his instinct down the road.

CHAPTER TWENTY-ONE
WILL

Will was locked in a small room, only about ten feet wide by ten feet long. The floor was carpeted, all four walls painted a slate blue—more than likely somebody's office in the previous world. Now, it was empty aside from the prisoner. Above his head, built into the wall he sat against, was a window that brought in the pale light of the overcast day.

Jonas had restrained from roughing Will up more when he put him in the room, instead only tying his hands and stuffing a dirty sock in his mouth before leaving him sitting on the floor, alone.

Will suspected that Holly might be in a similar situation to his, perhaps even in the next room over. Clearly, David Ellis wanted full control of his camp. A disobedient flame like Holly would need to be extinguished for him to keep it.

Outside the door, Will heard footsteps. A door creaked open just down the hall from where he was entrapped. He heard the muted panic of a woman who sounded like she was gagged the same way he was.

Holly.

Will listened as her shrieks got louder before progressively fading. He closed his eyes so he could concentrate on her voice and estimate how far away they were taking her until her voice disappeared.

Then Will heard footsteps again. This time, they stopped in front of his room. He heard a click and then looked up to see the door open.

David's eyes glared at him.

For a moment, he just stood in the doorway and stared down at Will. It was an act of intimidation, which Will found almost comical at this point. He sat on the ground, blood dried at the mouth, staring back into David's determined eyes.

David entered the room, his boots clicking on the floor. He pulled a bowie knife from his pocket, which finally made Will stir.

"So you *are* afraid," David said, grinning, as he waved the knife inches from Will's face.

He pulled a cloth out of his pocket and began running it up and down the blade of the knife, cleaning it.

David knelt down with the knife in his hand, the blade pointed at Will, who began to squirm and yell through the sock. David reached toward him and pulled the sock from his mouth. Will gasped for air.

"I'm going to give you another chance," David said. "While I see you as a threat to my agenda, I think that you could be of very good use to my plans here, if you want to be. If you play by my rules."

Will caught his breath. Staring into the eyes of a man who had tried to feed him to the dead, he couldn't help but question the motive.

"I have family out there. I have to find them," Will said.

"You *think* you have family out there. But you don't know

for sure," David said. He pointed toward the front of the building. "For all you know, they could look like those ugly fucks outside by now."

Will's blood went cold. He glared at David, wanting nothing more than to snatch the knife from the psycho's hands and slash his throat.

"We can be your family, William," David said.

Will let out a 'pssh' noise and then looked away. He stared at the wall for a moment before looking back at him.

"Fuck you."

David let out a small laugh. He looked down at the knife. "Wrong answer."

He leaned in and put the knife to Will's throat, freezing when he heard the shouting behind him from another room.

"Who the hell is that?" the voice shouted.

David looked behind him, letting the cold blade stay rested against Will's throat. He looked back at Will and flashed him a smile

"I'll be back to finish this," David said, patting Will on his cheek.

He pulled the knife away from Will's neck, stood up, and left the room, leaving Will behind to think about how much time he possibly had left in his life.

***

In the bathroom across the hall, Marcus peeked through the crack in the door at the hinges, waiting for David to leave the room. Once he did, Marcus moved quickly into Will's room, being sure to quietly open the door and close it behind him, holding the handle down to prevent the loud click.

Will's eyes got wide when he saw Marcus. He began to

squirm and try to work his way out of the ropes again.

Marcus put his finger to his mouth, signaling for Will to hush. He walked over to him and pulled a knife out of his pocket.

Will pulled his head away, waiting for Marcus to take the knife to his throat.

"David send you in here to do his dirty work?" Will asked.

Marcus smiled. "Not exactly."

He reached behind Will and began to cut at the ropes with the knife.

"What the hell are you doing?" Will said.

"Shut up and listen," Marcus began. "Holly was right. That guy out there, that monster...that isn't the same David Ellis that I know." He kept sawing at the ropes. "We gotta get Holly and get the hell out of here."

"Where is she?" Will asked.

Marcus nodded toward the door. "They've got her out there, tied up like you. I think David aims to make an example out of the two of you."

The ropes came loose and Will took turns rubbing his wrists with his hands.

"Come on," Marcus said, offering Will a hand to help him get up. Will accepted, pulling himself up and almost falling, his legs fast asleep.

They went to the door and Marcus peeked out to make sure the hall was clear.

"We're gonna head to the right. We gotta make a quick stop before we can go get Holly. Follow me."

The door opened and they headed for the armory.

***

Enough of the Empties had scattered to other parts of the industrial park to allow time and open space for the SUV to park at the front of the building.

Jonas looked back to David as he entered the room.

"Some guy is out there with a kid. Apparently, he followed Rich and Mike back here. He's begging us for food and shelter," Jonas said.

David nodded at Jonas and walked to the end of the loading dock. He looked down the industrial park to his right and noticed that most of the Empties had gathered around a deer that had gotten loose in the area from the woods nearby. Only a couple of them gathered around the SUV with the man and child inside.

"What do you want?" David said.

"Food. Water. Anything that you can spare," Gabriel said. "I have a child with me."

David spit on the ground below. He pointed out to the west.

"You couldn't find any food out there?" David asked.

Gabriel shook his head. "Have you people been out there? Everything is being or has been looted. These *things*, they're blocking the paths into stores and homes."

David pulled out a cigarette and lit it, letting the smoke rise into the air above his face.

"I'm sorry," David said, pushing the smoke from his lungs. "But we can't help you. Now get the fuck outta here."

When David moved, Holly could be seen behind him, tied up and gagged.

"What the hell is going on in there?" Gabriel shouted.

David turned around. He pushed his coat aside and

178

pulled the gun from the holster at his side.

"Did you not fucking hear what I said?" David yelled.

He fired his pistol at Gabriel, whose eyes had gone wide upon the drawing of the gun, and David now watched him shield the young boy in the passenger seat as the window shattered.

The assault ended when gunshots rang behind David's head. He dived behind a pallet stacked with boxes of white copy paper.

When he looked up to see what was happening, Holly was snatched away by Will.

CHAPTER TWENTY-TWO

"Are you okay?" Gabriel asked Dylan.

The boy remained curled up in the seat, covering his ears and barely able to hear his own crying. The gunshot had startled him and made Gabriel wonder what kind of man could fire a gun into a vehicle with a child. But another problem was looming.

The gunshot had attracted a group of beasts, the deer no longer a distraction.

Gabriel looked in the back seat and noticed that the passenger side window was broken, matching the one in the front seat.

"Dylan, you need to move to the seat behind me, okay?"

The boy didn't move. He remained balled up, ears covered.

"Dylan! Dylan!" Gabriel shouted.

Finally, the boy looked up. He nodded hesitantly, worked himself out of his ball, and moved to the back seat, behind Gabriel and away from the open windows.

Gabriel threw the truck into *Drive* and screamed as he floored the gas pedal, running over three of the creatures before turning the truck around to exit the industrial park.

As he passed back by the bay doors of the warehouse, he saw and heard, gunfire moving in both directions. Then, he saw it. Beside the building, sitting behind a chain link fence, he saw the same white car he'd spent the better part of the morning chasing.

Gabriel shook his head, sighed, and hit the gas pedal, heading out of the industrial park.

***

"Man down! Man down!" Jonas yelled.

David sat on the concrete, his back against a pallet of brown boxes filled with industrial shrink wrap. He checked his body for wounds, not sure if he had been hit.

"We don't want to hurt anyone! We just want to talk to David!" Will called out.

"It's too late for that!" Jonas yelled, trying to stop the bleeding on Leon's stomach.

"No one else needs to get hurt, Jonas!" Marcus called out.

David's face went dark. He turned and looked over the pallet.

"Traitor!" he screamed out.

Marcus leaned against the wall and shook his head. He looked at Holly.

"Do you know how many people are here?"

No longer tied up or gagged, Holly thought for a moment. "Two men are outside guarding the gate. And then there should be eight more in here," she said. "Well, seven." She was thinking of Leon, lying on his back and possibly bleeding out from the gunshot wound to the stomach.

"David!" Marcus shouted out. "Leon fired at us first. I can promise you that we don't want to hurt anyone. We just want out of here."

David grabbed an assault rifle leaning against a wall a few yards away from him. He checked the clip to confirm it was loaded. David slipped the clip back in, pushing gently enough to lock it in place but still control the volume of the click it made. Jonas was knelt down behind a pallet beside him and David nodded at him. Jonas looked over to Mike and Rich, signaling them.

"We're past that, Marcus! No one is leaving!" David said.

Marcus closed his eyes and banged his head against the wall three times. He wondered if he had made a mistake turning against David, trusting the word of Holly that Will could be trusted.

"Please, David! Don't do this!" Marcus pleaded.

Will looked over at Marcus.

"I don't think he's going to give us a choice." He looked over at Holly and then back to Marcus. "It's us or them."

Marcus nodded at Will.

David lowered his eyebrows as he heard the roaring engine outside. He looked through the loading dock door and saw the black SUV scream down the hill toward the building.

Jonas grabbed the radio from his side and began to yell into it.

"Guard the fence! Incoming!"

Then they heard the crash through the fence and the gunfire ensued outside.

CHAPTER TWENTY-THREE

Five minutes earlier...

"We have to go back! We can't leave them!" Dylan begged.

Gabriel kept his eyes on the road as the truck pulled back onto the highway. Part of him knew the boy was right, but he wasn't prepared to go vigilante and try to help some people he didn't know. His guilt kept him from responding to the boy.

They passed abandoned car after abandoned car and saw creatures lurking along the highway, the truck veering left and right to avoid them while Gabriel ignored the boy.

"Please! Go back!"

Gabriel stopped the truck on the shoulder and banged his head against the steering wheel. His conscience was catching up to him and he knew what the right thing to do was. He looked back to Dylan.

"That's what you want?" Gabriel asked Dylan.

The boy nodded.

Three beasts approached the truck

Gabriel reached into the back seat and grabbed the baseball bat out of the duffle bag. He held it in his hands for a moment, feeling the comfort of the grip, before pulling his right hand off to confirm the gun was mounted to his side.

Again, he looked back to Dylan.

"Then we do it my way."

***

Drew Hilton took his hand off the end of the assault rifle for just a moment so he could pull the cigarette out of his mouth and exhale the toxins into the air. As commanded, he stood inside the fenced area at the side of the building, guarding the door in case Marcus, Will, and Holly tried to make a run for it. Four Empties clawed and gripped the fence, howling at him to open it. He shook his head.

"Ugly mother fuckers."

He sat on the hood of the white hatchback while facing the door to the building. The cigarette burned down to the butt and Drew flicked it onto the ground with the others.

As he blew the last cloud of smoke from his lungs, he heard a noise in the distance getting louder. Drew stood and walked toward the fence.

His eyes widened as the black SUV came into view around the corner, and it was coming right at him.

Drew locked the rifle into his hip, pulled the trigger, and began to fire at the oncoming truck.

It didn't stop.

His radio began to scream at his side.

"Guard the fence! Incoming!" Jonas shouted through the walkie.

"Shit!" Drew yelled, diving out of the way.

The SUV stormed toward the gate, launching two of the beasts into the chain link as it knocked it down.

***

The sound of the SUV crashing through the fence blew

through the warehouse, and David's group took it as their opportunity to try and catch the three rebels off guard.

Rich and Mike left their post and ran to the edge of the room, firing down the hallway toward Will, Marcus, and Holly.

Marcus was exposed, but quickly took cover behind the corner just as the men began to fire at them. He leaned against the wall and caught his breath. They were at the end of a long hallway. David had three men with him, one injured, a man outside, and the two women in the group were likely holed away in an office hiding.

Holly's hand shook on the grip of the gun. She was holding a lightweight assault rifle and the barrel waved through the air.

"We need you, Holly," Will said. "Just breathe."

She closed her eyes and held a solemn grip on the gun.

Marcus turned his head around the corner again and Rich fired another shot, barely missing. He looked to Will.

"Give me some cover."

Will let the assault rifle sit at his hip, the strap hanging over his shoulder, as he drew the pistol from his side. He reached his hand around the corner and began to fire, sending Mike and Rich behind a stack of boxes.

Marcus let out a breath and ran down the hallway into one of the side rooms, unseen by any of the men.

David, still sitting behind the pallet of boxes, signaled Jonas to join his two comrades. Jonas nodded, stood, and ran toward them, firing down the hall to cover himself.

Will and Holly were on opposite sides of the hallway. In order for them to move to where they needed to go, Holly would have to get across the opening to Will's side.

"I'm gonna cover you," Will said.

Holly was shaking again. Tears came running from her eyes.

"It's gonna be okay. They won't be able to shoot at you with me firing at them."

She gently nodded her head.

Will counted down from five.

"Now!"

Will pointed his pistol down the hall and fired. Holly waited and ran across the hall. Jonas pointed a gun up over the boxes and shot, the bullet arriving just behind Holly and going into the wall. She fell to the ground.

"Come on!" Will said, leaning over to pick her up. They hurried down the hall.

David stood and the men were silent. They could hear the footsteps hurrying down the hall. He pointed that way.

"After them!"

**

Gabriel opened the door to the SUV and saw the man he had nearly run over lying face down on the concrete. He walked over and nudged Drew with his foot; he didn't move. Looking to his left, Gabriel saw two more beasts appear ten yards away from the gate. Through a radio on the man's hip, Gabriel heard someone shouting, "Drew? Are you there?"

When he turned to point the gun at them, a boot hit Gabriel in the side of the knee, sending him to the ground. The gun flew out of his hand as he grimaced, writhing on the ground.

Drew pounced on Gabriel, landing two initial punches to

his face while he had him off guard. Gabriel got his hands up, grabbing Drew's shirt, and was able to block further punches.

When Drew reached for the pistol, Gabriel brought his right hand off of Drew's shoulder and landed a punch right below his left eye. The blow sent Drew rolling off of him and he landed directly on top of his gun.

Gabriel rolled over onto his knees and lunged at Drew just as he pulled out the pistol. Gabriel hit his arm, forcing the bullet wide, under him instead of through him.

He shifted his weight onto Drew, pinning the arm with the gun down to the ground as they fought each other with their other arms.

Gabriel lost his balance and leaned too far into Drew, who took the chance to deliver a head butt to Gabriel, the crack of his nose ringing in Drew's ear.

Drew stumbled to his feet, his back to the fence, and looked down at Gabriel. He wiped blood away from his mouth, smiling as he looked down at the iron substance on the back of his hand.

Gabriel just stared through Drew, supporting himself on his right elbow and holding his left arm up, surrendering.

Drew smiled. He brought the handgun up and pointed it down between Gabriel's eyes. "You lose," Drew said.

Gabriel tensed his body and closed his eyes.

Two creatures pulled Drew down from behind, just as he was about to pull the trigger. He got one shot off, but it sang through the air, flying over the building. They followed him to the ground, pouncing on his face.

Gabriel watched the scene in horror as Drew drowned

under the bodies, waving his arms in the air and pleading for help. He listened to the terror in the man's final screams.

The gun was pinned under the undead; there would be no getting it. Gabriel had mistakenly placed the shotgun he had gotten at the sporting goods store in the very back part of the SUV, and with the beasts lurking, had no time to grab it. Gabriel saw the baseball bat lying in the front seat. He reached through the door and grabbed it, the cannibal distracted with the fresh meal of living flesh.

Gabriel opened the door to the warehouse as the screaming stopped, confirming the beasts had done their job with no need for him to look back.

***

The rest of the warehouse became eerily quiet as the three men ran down the hall after the rebels. David could hear the echo of the click of his boots as he got to his feet. He walked to the center of the room just as Marcus came around the corner pointing a pistol at him.

David returned the favor, bringing his gun up to eye level with Marcus.

The two men stared at each other, each moving to their right.

Marcus spoke first.

"We don't have to do this, David."

David smiled. He cocked his head to the side, the joints in his neck cracking, which he followed with a shoulder shrug.

"It's too late. It's done." David continued to shuffle to the side. "What do you think is going to happen when they find that piece of shit and that traitor bitch?" David asked, speaking of Will and Holly.

Sweat dripped down Marcus' cheek. He didn't want to shoot David. The two had been friends for years and when times had been tough for him, David had given him an opportunity to start over. In this tense stare down, looking down the barrel of a gun, Marcus remembered this, and guilt came over him.

Slowly, Marcus let his arm fall to the side. He knelt down, never letting his eyes leave David's, and set the gun on the concrete floor of the warehouse. Straightening his knees, he lifted his hands to the air.

"Come on, David. Let's just talk."

Keeping his hands up, Marcus began to move toward David.

"Put the gun down, David. We can end this."

David laughed. He waved the gun in the air like he was leading an orchestra through Beethoven's 9th *Symphony*.

"End this?" David scoffed. "End this? The end is here, Marcus." He pointed to the open loading dock door. "Look outside!"

His reaction was to follow David's movements and look outside, and when he did, David fired.

Marcus stepped back, shocked by the sudden impact, and clutched the right side of his chest right below his collarbone. He looked at David and fell to the ground, landing on his rear and holding himself up with his left palm while his right continued to try and stop the bleeding from the black hole in his chest.

David took his time approaching Marcus. He let his eyes leave him to look outside and watch the Empties move aimlessly around the parking lot. The vastness of how much the world had changed hit him in this moment. Outside, people roamed, void of any soul or thought. And though he could still put together coherent thoughts, he felt that perhaps his own soul had passed. He'd come to a place where one of his best friends was bleeding from a gunshot wound that he'd inflicted himself. The moment saddened him, but only briefly, before his cold desire for power crept back in.

He stared down at Marcus, whose eyes were glazing over.

"Who the hell are you?" Marcus asked.

From the back of the building, there was an explosion that shook the floor, causing David to lose his balance, but not quite enough of a shock for him to fall. He smiled, sure that his soldiers had carried out their duty and ended the rebellion in a swift manner.

He looked at Marcus and gave him a grim, cold smile.

David cocked the pistol.

"I am the devil."

Footsteps were followed by a scream behind him, and right as David turned, a wooden baseball bat connected with the side of his neck, sending him down to the ground. He was out cold.

Marcus looked up and stared into Gabriel's eyes.

David lay between them in the fetal position, not moving.

Gabriel gripped the bat with both hands, staring down at the black man bleeding from his chest.

Marcus reached for the pistol, his eyes wide, and aimed it past Gabriel.

"Duck!" Marcus yelled.

Gabriel abided, falling to the ground just as a bullet went over him.

Marcus aimed the gun into David's office, fired, and watched the glass shatter as Diane Baldwin, one of David's other loyals, fell back, the bullet having hit her in the chest near her heart. She fell out of sight.

Gabriel uncovered his head and looked up at Marcus.

"Thanks," he said.

Marcus nodded. The adrenaline abated and the realization of his wound returned as he rolled down on his side, grimacing.

Gabriel crouched over Marcus, assessing the wound.

"You need a doctor. Bad."

Marcus let out a chirping laugh.

"No shit," he responded with a smile.

Footsteps echoed down the hall and Gabriel took the gun from Marcus, pointing it that way.

Will came around the corner, his weapon ready, and the two men pointed at each other.

Marcus looked back and forth between Will and Gabriel.

"Whoa, whoa, whoa!" Marcus looked at Will. "It's okay, he's with us," he said, looking at Gabriel.

Will lowered his weapon and, moments later, Gabriel did the same.

Holly joined them, walking out from behind Will as they entered the room. She saw Marcus lying on the ground and rushed to his side.

"Oh, God. What happened?" she asked.

A towel sat on top of a box on the other end of the room, and Holly rushed over and grabbed it. She ran back to Marcus, knelt down, and pressed the towel over the wound as he yelled from the initial pressure.

Will looked down and saw David out cold next to them. He tipped his head at him.

"Is he dead?" Will asked.

Gabriel reached down and grabbed David's wrist, checking his pulse.

He shook his head. "It's faint, but he's there." Then Gabriel looked at Marcus again before bringing his eyes back to Will. "He needs a doctor. He's losing a lot of blood."

"I can help."

The voice came from behind them and Will turned, pointing his gun at the woman across the room.

She raised her hands.

It was Miranda, the other woman in David's group.

Will lowered his gun.

She walked over to them, keeping her hands raised to show her innocence. That she was unarmed.

"I was a nurse before I started working for this prick," Miranda said, nodding her head at the unconscious David on the floor.

Will looked to Gabriel and Marcus.

"Whatever we are gonna do, we need to do it fast. We blew the back of this building with a grenade during a shoot-out. It took down a wall to the outside and it wouldn't surprise me if it attracted some of the Empties."

Gabriel squinted his face. "Empties?"

Will shook his head. "I'll explain later. You got a way for us to get out of here?"

Gabriel pointed to the side of the building. "There's a door that leads out to the side. I've got an SUV that we should all be able to squeeze into. Some of those things.

Empties, you said? They're probably out there. I'll have to jumpstart the truck." He looked around to the guns. "But I think we can take 'em out and get him to the truck," he said, nodding at Marcus.

"Who are you?" Will asked.

Gabriel stood. He tilted his head down slightly and extended his hand to Will.

"Gabriel. Gabriel Alexander."

Will took his hand. "Will Kessler."

"Well, Will," Gabriel said. "Whatever we are gonna do, we need to do it."

"Did you say you have to jumpstart your truck?" Marcus asked.

Gabriel nodded.

Marcus reached into his pocket, pulled out his keys, and then threw them to Will. "Let's take mine. It's the white Escalade parked all the way to the back of that fenced-in area."

Simultaneously, Will and Gabriel nodded.

"What about him?" Holly asked, looking down at David.

Before Will could respond, Marcus did.

"Leave him."

They looked at Marcus, and Will nodded, a sign of respect because he knew he had been close to David at one time. The words could not have come easily out of the injured man's mouth.

Will looked over to Gabriel and smiled.

"You're gonna need more than a bat."

Gabriel returned the grin. "Nah, it's more fun this way."

***

193

There were Empties outside—six of them, to be exact. Gabriel and Will opened the door and cleared the path to the SUV, taking the Empties out one by one, while Miranda and Holly tended to Marcus just inside the building

Will looked to Gabriel.

"I'm going to pull the truck up here. Run inside and see if you can help them get Marcus out here."

Gabriel nodded, heading back into the warehouse while Will jogged the ten yards to Marcus' truck.

A few moments later, the three able-bodies appeared at the door, supporting Marcus. They loaded him onto the back seat of the SUV. Miranda joined him in the back, while Holly sat in the trunk area behind the back seat.

Gabriel looked at Will.

"Mind if I drive?"

Will shook his head.

The engine turned over as more Empties were beginning to make their way past the fallen gate.

Gabriel threw the truck into reverse and backed over two of the Empties. Marcus grimaced from the bumpy ride of passing over the bodies.

"Sorry," Gabriel said, watching behind him through the rearview mirror.

"Where are we headed?" Will asked Gabriel.

"I gotta make a pit stop. I left something in a stranded vehicle on the highway."

"Then where?"

Gabriel didn't respond.

When the truck pulled through the fence and into the parking lot, he cut the wheel and whipped it around.

As Gabriel put it in drive, Will took one last look to the end of the road at Element. He saw Empties walking off the edge of the loading dock and falling face-first to the concrete, having gone in through the front door, scavenging for life that wasn't there.

For a moment, the truck sat in front of David Ellis' building—which had smoke rising into the air behind it, from the fire at the back of it. Through the back window Holly could see David still lying on the floor in the center of the warehouse.

She didn't smile for him. She only watched him lay still as the truck pulled away.

CHAPTER TWENTY-FOUR

After they picked up Dylan from the abandoned car Gabriel had left him in on the highway, they pulled off one of the exits a couple of miles down the road and found an empty quick lube shop at the top of a small hill, a space with no Empties around. Gabriel pulled the SUV inside and they shut the garage doors.

Will looked back at Holly, who was leaning over the back seat and running her hands across the top of Marcus' head. Dylan had joined her back there and had instantly taken a liking to Holly, which was good, because she seemed to be good with kids and the boy needed a distraction to stay calm.

"How is he?" Will asked, looking at Miranda.

"He's lost a lot of blood. He's lucky. It looks like the bullet missed all his organs. For the moment, I've suppressed the bleeding, but he's still in rough shape. But for now, I think he can just rest."

Will nodded. He reached into his bag, grabbed his cell phone, and then looked over to Gabriel and gave him a nod toward the door, asking him to join him outside of the SUV.

They got out and stepped a few feet in front of the truck. The garage smelled like old, settled motor oil. Like the place hadn't been used in over a decade. On a table nearby, there was a dust-covered packet of chewing tobacco and a black-stained work shirt thrown over a chair. The name patch still showed and read "Ricky" in cursive red letters.

Gabriel bobbed his head toward the pouch of chewing tobacco. "Wish that was a pack of cigarettes."

Will smiled. "I quit a year ago. Just not worth it, ya know?"

"Would be right about now."

"Thanks a lot for what you did back there."

"Don't mention it."

"So, what now?"

Gabriel slipped his hands into the pockets of his athletic pants and hopped on his tip-toes for a moment, trying to stay warm.

"I'm headed to Washington D.C. My wife and daughter are there and so is the boy's family."

"Have you spoken with them?"

Gabriel sighed and just looked to the ground.

"I'll be glad to take you guys anywhere you need along the way. But I've got to get there."

Will nodded.

Gabriel looked down at the phone. "That thing work? I wouldn't mind making a call. I lost my phone in the plane crash."

Will cocked his head. "You were in that crash?"

Gabriel nodded. "We were the only two survivors," he said, looking at Dylan.

"Shit," Will said.

"So, does it work?"

Will shrugged. "I wasn't getting a signal before. I just turned it off to save power."

He pressed his thumb against the power button at the top

and watched the black light brighten as the phone began to boot.

While he waited, Gabriel peeked around the garage. He put his hand on a stack of old used tires, the tread almost completely washed away from the one on top. On the wall was a calendar with a gorgeous blonde wearing a bikini that looked to be a size too small, minimum. Gabriel walked to it and checked the month: *July 2011.*

As he turned around, he kicked something. He looked down and his eyes lit up. Two red, metal gas cans lay at his feet, and they didn't budge when he kicked them. He leaned over, picking up the first one and finding it half full. The second was almost three-quarters of the way full. Down on one knee, he unscrewed the cap, releasing the smell of pure, unleaded fuel into the air. He walked both cans in a farmer's carry back to the SUV.

Will looked over. "Oh, shit. They full?"

"Almost."

"Thank God."

"Anything yet?"

"It finished booting, but no service yet."

Will waited, licking his lips as he stared at the corner of the screen, hoping that the words *No Service* would be replaced with tiny, ascending columns.

Then the phone beeped, which made Gabriel approach and look over Will's shoulder.

Multiple missed calls appeared, all from the same number Will didn't recognize. It had an *865* area code.

"Do you know anyone in Knoxville?" Gabriel asked. He knew the area code from having had to call on clients there in the past.

Will shook his head. He pressed a few keys on the phone and re-dialed the number. It took almost no time for the phone to beep at him. He tried two more times with the same result. Disappointment: that's what covered his face.

"Sorry, man," Gabriel said, sincerely. He felt the timing might be a little too quick, but he asked anyway, "Mind if I try to reach my wife and daughter?"

Keeping his eyes to the floor, Will shook his head and handed the phone to Gabriel.

"Thanks."

Gabriel couldn't dial the number fast enough. Every moment since that crash he'd thought of his wife and daughter. Begged and pleaded to hear their voices, to see them again. He rounded his lips with his tongue, moistening them and tasting the salt from the sweat, then bit his bottom lip.

The phone rang once and he gasped.

Then a busy signal.

Frantically, he tried again. And again. And once more. All with the same result.

Will felt his disappointment. "Sorry, bro."

Gabriel handed him the phone and went to the other side of the room, and then sat on a small, black stool with wheels. He put his face in his hands and Will allowed him to be alone.

As Will went to slip the phone into the back pocket of his jeans, it chirped. He looked at the lit screen and read: *1 New Text Message*. After sliding his thumb across the screen, the message appeared:

199

Will, it's your mother. I can't reach you. I want you to know that I am ok. Your father and I went to a hotel in the North Carolina mountains. Things got crazy. With a girl now and headed to Knoxville. I hope to see you soon. Love you.

Will went to his knees, clutched the phone to his chest, and wept.

EPILOGUE

Two days later...

Down Interstate 40, abandoned cars lined the road and bodies lay bathing in the sun, still warm, though winter was steadfastly approaching. Many of the bodies had begun to decay; their flesh had been picked from the bone by the Empty bodies, which still limped up and down the highway, aimlessly looking for more life to devour.

Lawrence sped down the highway, swerving to miss dead bodies and looking into the faces of the creeping death that wandered on the open road. Every day he did this and every day he had hope that he would find more survivors.

He worked his normal route, scared to veer from it due to the fear of what he might see. In the new world, the familiar was your friend.

The world had changed. And for Lawrence Holloway, the adaptation to his sudden new responsibility still overwhelmed him.

It was the first day in three that it hadn't rained. The reemergence of the sun brought at least a little bit of joy into his day.

It had been a few days since Lawrence last found any survivors. Day after day of driving into the sleeping world without a hint of life had begun to wear thin on him.

Then in the distance, he saw something. It was a different movement. Not so much unlike the dead lurkers who moved unbalanced down the road, but also not much like them.

More like him.

He pressed the gas, moving the ambulance down the road with haste.

It came to a stop next to the ditch, and one look confirmed exactly what Lawrence had hoped. It was a man. A living, breathing man. He had fallen off the shoulder and was lying on his back, his nose to the sun and eyes closed.

Lawrence rolled down the window.

"Hello?" he yelled.

The man didn't move.

Lawrence jumped out of the ambulance. Forty yards away, four beasts weaved in and out of abandoned cars toward them. He ran to the man's side and began to shake him.

"Wake up. I'm here to help you," Lawrence said.

The man opened his eyes and brought his hands around Lawrence's neck.

Lawrence gasped for air.

"Here to help you," Lawrence said through faint breath.

The man loosened his grip, realizing that Lawrence wasn't one of the undead.

Lawrence held his throat and gasped for his breath.

"I'm sorry," the drifter said. "I thought you were one of them."

Lawrence continued to writhe, shaking his head and waving the man off as if to say it was okay. He caught his breath.

"Are you wounded?" Lawrence said with a hoarse voice.

"Sort of," the man said. "I'm mainly just hungry. Tired."

The beasts were gaining ground, the position of the cars

buying the men a little time.

Lawrence looked to them.

"Yeah, well, so are they. So unless you wanna be their lunch, I suggest that we get the hell out of here."

Lawrence extended his hand and the drifter took it.

Lawrence opened the back of the ambulance and helped the battered man inside. He shut the back doors, making sure the handles were locked in place, and hustled to the cockpit. The creatures were in front of him, but instead of running them over, he put the ambulance into reverse and gave himself enough space to turn around.

"Why didn't you just run them over?" the drifter asked.

Lawrence smiled and shrugged, staring at the blue eyes in the rearview mirror.

"Why would I do that? They were people. I wouldn't run over a grave if I didn't have to."

The drifter looked away, putting his hand to his lips.

"They aren't people anymore," he said.

Lawrence shook his head and kept his eyes on the road.

The drifter reached to his side and wrapped his hand around the grip of the knife on his waist.

"Where are you taking me?"

Lawrence smiled and looked into the mirror again. "East. I'm taking you east. There's a hospital there. It's sort of become a refugee camp of sorts for survivors. We can get you checked out there, along with some food and a place to rest your head."

The drifter let go of the knife and loosened the muscles in his face. The thoughts of slitting Lawrence's throat and driving off with the ambulance went away. He wanted to see this hospital. This refugee camp.

"My name's Lawrence. What's yours, stranger?"

The drifter brought his hands together and rubbed them clean of the weapon. He looked into the mirror and smiled back at the young driver.

"Ellis. David Ellis."

TO BE CONTINUED...

Want to be the first to know when the next book is coming out?

Join my new release mailing list and receive a free eBook at:

www.zachbohannon.com

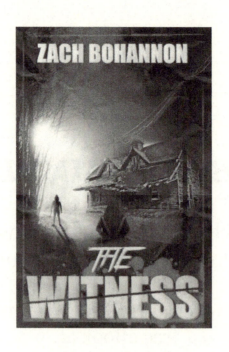

THE WITNESS
A Slasher Novel

For fans of *Friday the 13th*, *The Texas Chainsaw Massacre*, *House of 1,000 Corpses*, and *Halloween*

Available Now!

Visit: http://bit.ly/witnessbook

For independent authors like myself, reviews are very important. They help new readers discover our work so that they can enjoy our stories and we can write more books.

If you enjoyed this book, I would be forever grateful if you would take the time to leave a review on the website you purchased it to help other readers.

And if you have any questions or comments regarding this title or anything else for that matter, I'd love to hear from you. Please feel free to e-mail me at info@zachbohannon.com.

ACKNOWLEDGEMENTS

Thank you, J. Thorn, for your fun, engaging storytelling, and for your guidance, feedback, and friendship along the way.

Taylor Krauss, thank you for your honest, detailed feedback, and for your friendship.

To my beta readers, Meghan Cowhan and Joe Orozco. Thank you for agreeing to read the work of a new author that you never heard of and providing valuable feedback.

Thank you, Johnny Digges, for the amazing cover designs. It's crazy how we have been friends since we were ten years old, and it's come from us playing hockey together to doing this!

Thank you, Jennifer Collins, for not only your amazing edits and proofreads, but for coaching me along the way.

And a shout to my fellow horror author friends, Dan Padavona and David J. Delaney, who I've had wonderful conversations with about writing, reading, marketing, Australia, and metal.

AUTHOR'S NOTE

If I were to be truly honest with you, I would tell you that I had no desire to write a zombie book.

Really.

I'd wanted to write a post-apocalyptic book for a long time. I started a couple of different ones, including one that was eerily like Hugh Howey's best-selling opus, *Wool*. I'm not comparing the two, believe me. Hugh is a much better writer than I am, and *Wool* is an amazing story. But the premise was very similar (my characters lived in an underground city called The Gulch, much like the Silos in *Wool*).

So how did *Empty Bodies* come about if I didn't want to write a zombie novel?

When I was writing the stories for *Dark Reveries: Volume One,* I decided that, while I didn't want to write a whole novel about zombies, it would be fun to write a short story about them. So I took a simple scenario that was close to me.

For my full-time job, I work as the warehouse manager for a popular cymbal and percussion manufacturer, and our 50,000 square foot facility is located in an industrial park that dead ends just past our building. Everyday I have a couple of employees who take naps on their lunch break in one of our extra offices. One day I thought to myself: *What if some of the employees turned into zombies while one of those guys was fast asleep in that office?* And with that, the short story *Warehouse 3427* was born.

The story was more fun to write than I thought it was going to be. The plot kept growing and I found myself sitting in the chair, not able to stop writing.

Before I knew it, I had written over 10,000 words, and knew that I had a lot more story to tell. I thought of other characters and finally convinced myself that I had a novel.

Then once I started planning the book, I quickly realized I didn't have a novel. I had at least three, maybe more.

Thus, now you hold the first book in the *Empty Bodies* series.

I really hope that you enjoyed the story. Will, Jessica, and Gabriel were a lot of fun to write, and I can't wait to tell you more about their journeys!

I'm already working on the second book, and if you want to be the first to know when it will be coming out, please visit www.zachbohannon.com. Also, please consider sending me an e-mail and letting me know what you thought of the story. I'd love to hear from you! My e-mail is info@zachbohannon.com.

Thanks again for reading!

-ZBB

ABOUT THE AUTHOR

Something about the dark side of life has always appealed to me. Whether I experience it through reading and watching horror or listening to my favorite heavy metal bands, I have been forever fascinated with the shadow of human emotion.

While in my 20's, I discovered my passion to create through playing drums in two heavy metal bands: Kerygma and Twelve Winters. While playing in Twelve Winters (a power metal band with a thrash edge fronted by my now wife Kathryn), I was able to indulge myself in my love of writing by penning the lyrics for all our music. My love of telling a story started here, as many of the songs became connected to the same concept and characters in one way or another.

Now in my 30's, my creative passion is being passed to

willing readers through the art of stories. While I have a particular fascination for real life scenarios, I also love dark fantasy. So, you'll find a little bit of everything in my stories, from zombies to serial killers, angels and demons to mindless psychopaths, and even ghosts and parallel dimensions.

My influences as a writer come primarily from the works of Clive Barker, Stephen King, and Blake Crouch in the written form; the beautifully dark, rich lyrics of Mikael Akerfeldt from the band Opeth; and an array of movies, going back to the root of my fascination at a young age with 70's and 80's slasher films such as *Halloween, Friday the 13th,* and *The Texas Chainsaw Massacre.*

I live in Nashville, Tennessee with my wife Kathryn, our daughter Haley, and our German Shepherd Guinness. When I'm not writing, I enjoy playing hockey, watching hockey and football, cycling, watching some of my favorite television shows and movies, and, of course, reading.

Connect with me online:

Website: www.zachbohannon.com
Facebook: http://www.facebook.com/zbbwrites
Pinterest: http://www.pinterest.com/zbbwrites
Twitter: @zachbohannon32
Instagram: @zachbohannon

KEEP ON READING!

For a complete list of Zach Bohannon's books,
please visit:

www.zachbohannon.com

Made in the USA
Monee, IL
02 August 2020